TRAIL OF THE NIGHTSTALKERS

In among the trees, Ash Tamerlane found the man he'd shot lying belly-down. He swung to the ground and stared without pity at the wounded outlaw, who stirred at Tamerlane's presence.

"Mister, you busted me up bad."

"Just sending back some of your calling cards. You were heading to that mine. Where is it?"

The nightstalker seemed to see some dark humor in Tamerlane's question. "You'll never find it. And soon you'll be dead, same as me—" His head lolled to one side and he went limp.

"About the only way to kill a rattler is to cut off its head!" Tamerlane said grimly. He mounted up, and with the wind pushing at his back, a vengeful Ash Tamerlane began pushing hard upon the track of the nightstalkers.

THE UNTAMED WEST
brought to you by Zebra Books

ROBERT KAMMEN
MONTANA SHOWDOWN

ZEBRA BOOKS
KENSINGTON PUBLISHING CORP.

ZEBRA BOOKS

are published by

Kensington Publishing Corp.
475 Park Avenue South
New York, NY 10016

First printing: April, 1988

Printed in the United States of America

ONE

The lone horseman knew he'd made a fatal mistake by attempting to cross the Tobacco Roots tonight.

Then, as a jagged bolt of lightning tore the sky apart over the pass, highwayman Reno Lamont's steel-gray bronc went stifflegged and began bucking and snorting fear out of its flaring nostrils. Lamont clung as best he could to the saddle while trying to rein his crazed and bucking bronc away from the dropoff side of the trail. Somehow he brought his horse under control.

"Now, dammit, behave!" he snarled to the horse trembling under him.

The rain came down harder, fiercer than any spring storm had a right to do, and so bitterly cold that Reno Lamont hunkered wetly into his yellow slicker, rainwater pouring down the brim of his creased hat.

He wasn't a man inclined to fret about his past, sordid as it had been. The fear eeling at his mind came not from the storm, but from the sure knowledge he was being followed. Though the highwayman hadn't caught a glimpse of anyone since leaving Bannack, and

5

this despite backtrailing at times, he knew someone was back there. Now the bronc wheeled sideways when thunder boxcarred overhead to rattle eastward among blackish clouds.

Lashing out with the ends of his reins, he said, "Get a'movin', hoss."

He brought his bronc higher along this seldom-traveled canyon. If the highwayman had had his say about it, he would have used the main route further to the south to cross over the Tobacco Roots and into Virginia City. But he'd witnessed at close hand what had happened to others of his unlawful craft who'd disobeyed orders; either a bullet in the back or being manacled hand and ankle and taken to the hidden gold mine, there to be worked to death under the uncaring eyes of men brandishing bullwhips or lengths of chain. Despite himself, Reno Lamont shivered inwardly, that sense of unease burning at his belly, causing pain to spasm across his chest.

At first the highwayman wasn't clear what had happened. At the sound of someone moaning so strong and close he glanced wildly around, certain he'd also heard the bang of a handgun. Then it registered in Reno Lamont's mind that *he'd* done the moaning, with his hand going to his right shoulder to find blood staining it, and suddenly he felt weaker, couldn't stop the whining noise passing through his trembling lips.

"Far enough, Lamont!"

The highwayman swung his horse that way, and there, standing on a huge flat-topped boulder nudged against the cliff wall, was the man who'd shot him. There was no way, with his shoulder wound, that

Lamont could go for the revolver at his right hip, nor the Winchester sheathed further down, and he cried out, "All I've got is about . . . fifty bucks on me—"

In the sudden stab of lightning a clearer outline was revealed to the highwayman of a tall, slim-hipped man. Rainwater whipped about by the gusting wind shone off the man's shaggy mane of brownish hair showing under a hat tugged low over icy-gray eyes. He wore the gear of a cowhand, but no chaps. About the man who'd just wounded Reno Lamont was a calm, deliberate manner. The light faded away some, but stirring in the mind of the highwayman was a memory chord.

"Dammit," he said desperately, and through gritted teeth, "take my money and clear out!" The urge to throw up was strong in Lamont, and the shoulder was beginning to hurt.

"I don't want your money, Lamont."

Again, and under the seething clouds, poured down fiery light. And now the armed man stepped closer, some ten yards away, so that the highwayman could see the stubble of beard on the longish, gaunt face, and what appeared to be either scars or embedded marks trailing up alongside the left eye socket. Holstering his Deane-Adams, the stranger swept his unbuttoned rain slicker out of the way, and grasping both sides of his open shirt collar, he tore the shirt open. Of their own volition the highwayman's eyes went to the matted hair on the chest and stomach and to livid scarrings that could only have been made by a chain.

"You? But you're dead? I . . . I seen you fall over that cliff—"

"I'm still alive, damn you."

7

Down in Nevada the highwayman had known this man better'n he knew the countenance of the moon, but as someone to be treated with contempt, one of those who'd been sent down into the gold mines to labor away until they dropped from starvation or a link of chain done them in.

"Ash . . . that's it . . . you're Ash Tamerlane!"

"To my friends I am, you sonofabitch. You called me Chain, remember? Left your calling card on my chest . . . and face."

"No!" screamed the highwayman as he dug spurs into the flanks of his horse, and as the bronc surged uptrail, a slug from the Deane-Adams found Lamont's thigh. Toppling out of the saddle, he hit the gravelly track with a splash. He clawed around with his left hand for his gun, only to jab desperate fingers at an empty holster.

Then the one called Chain stood over the highwayman. The muzzle of his revolver was pointed at Reno Lamont's gaping eyes, the ominous clicking of its hammer being drawn back pounding terror deep into them.

"Killing you, Lamont, would be a pleasure. But all you are is a jackal. Ever see one? I did, once upon a long ago time in Africa. A jackal cleans up the leavings of the lion and tiger. Which pretty much describes you, Lamont."

"Please . . . please don't kill me—" He could feel a strange tightness engulfing his heaving chest; pain jackhammered at his heart.

"You're only a jackal working for the Cartel! You're also one of those nightstalkers, Lamont. Why are you going to Virginia City on a night such as this? To carry a message, perhaps, or report to one of your bosses. Back in Nevada your bosses saw to it my father was killed so's he couldn't tell the law what he knew about them, the Cartel. But you, Lamont, you're not important enough to know about them. In Virginia City are some, I suspect, mixed up in this bloody business. Who were you going to report to, Sheriff Henry Plummer? Yes, he's mixed up with the highwaymen, too, or so I suspect."

"Water . . . I need a drink—"

"Do like a turkey does on a rainy night—just tip your head back and open your lying mouth, Lamont."

The highwayman's sprawled frame shook as he began crying, at the pain of his wounds, and his fear of what was to come next. Lifting his left arm, he said piteously, "All of what you say . . . is true . . . Tamerlane."

"Truth comes hards to scum like you. Tell them when you get to Virginia City that the one called Chain is seeking those responsible for destroying my family. Tell them to shutter their windows at night and bolt their doors."

Suddenly the highwayman realized he was alone, and gasping deeply to rid himself of his fear, he tried pushing up from the rain-drenched trail. Upon coming to a sitting position, he spotted Ash Tamerlane bringing back his bronc. None too gently Tamerlane helped the wounded highwayman regain his saddle.

"We encounter one another again, Lamont, you're going down! Now ride, jackal!"

Ash Tamerlane triggered his revolver skyward to

have the bronc bolt away.

And next when lightning tracked glaringly down along this canyon passing over the Tobacco Roots, only the tracks of those who'd just been here remained, and with even these markings of the encounter between the highwayman and the one called Chain quickly being erased by the summery rainfall.

TWO

It was happenstance in the form of a depleted liquor supply, an empty bottle of Four Roses, that chanced to bring Frank O'Neal out of his room in the Commodore Hotel and down the broad staircase. The feisty Irishman was more accustomed to the room service one found back at the Biltmore in New York City, though he'd found a certain buccolic charm about the Commodore. While the gold-mining town of Virginia City, O'Neal had discovered after only a couple of weeks, was a lawless, roustering town thrust high upon the spiny ridge of the Bitter Roots.

O'Neal, of average height, and a man favoring tweed suits, a derby hat and flashy jewelry, had operated a detective agency just off Park Avenue in lower Manhattan. After his brazen attempt to blackmail a certain Tammany Hall politician had gone awry, Frank X. O'Neal found himself hotfooting out of town one step ahead of a bunco squad, his personal effects

11

in a carpetbag, the ten thousand he'd gotten from the politician in another. Upon arriving in Chicago, the first newspaper he picked up told of a gold strike out in territorial Montana. And being of shrewd and unsavory character, O'Neal caught another west-bound train. Another factor in the Irishman's decision to come here was the Civil War, now in its second bloody year. Most men his age, O'Neal was 32, had joined the armies of the cause they believed in. Another reason on O'Neal's part to head west had been the new inscription act just signed into law by President A. Lincoln. And since the Union Army could only send a token force out to man western outposts, it was highly unlikely the army or local lawmen would question the presence of another Irishman. Strangely enough, O'Neal, despite his New Yorkish ways, felt at home here.

He had a ruddy, thin-boned face adorned by a sandy-colored mustache. The brown derby was tilted cockily over closely-cropped hair, and, as was his habit, even for this mundane chore, Frank O'Neal's suit coat was buttoned properly, and with the wide tie trailing down the front of a boiled white shirt held in place by a diamond-studded clasp—any jeweler worth his salt would quickly determine it was merely cut glass. Appearances counted, even out here, O'Neal realized.

Down in the lobby sumptuously decorated with red velvet drapery, red-gaudy wallpaper and crystallized gas lanterns issuing soft yellowy light, O'Neal paused at the bottom of the staircase to gaze with avid curiosity at a couple who'd just entered. The woman's free-wheeling stride despite the bustled floor-length dress carried her across the lobby toward an arched doorway leading into the dining room. She was, O'Neal had learned, a woman of considerable means, if all of the bar talk was right, and recently come in by stagecoach. A silver dollar handed to one of the night clerks had produced the name Wyomia Blair. In Frank O'Neal's opinion she was the most beautiful woman to ever have graced the streets of Virginia City, or the whole territory for that matter. About the Blair woman was a melancholy aura, that not even the veil shielding her eyes could hide. The veil was attached to a black felt hat pinned to flowing chestnut hair.

A sudden onslaught of wind caused by the rainstorm assailing Virginia City brought O'Neal's eyes to a front window, then quickly back to the Blair woman wearing an Andalusia, a cape made of bluish velvety material and decorated with needlework and three-strand tassels. And, O'Neal recalled, the very latest fashion back east. The dress, though full, seemed to reveal rather than conceal Wyomia Blair's lissome figure. Conscious of Frank O'Neal's marked interest, she glanced his way, showing him heart-shaped ruby lips, and then she passed from view into the dining room.

"Tell me now?" questioned O'Neal. "What would a woman of such refinement be doing with a scamp such as that?" The man in question was much older, and a mountaineer, O'Neal deduced. Why, he didn't even have manners enough to doff his hat upon entering the dining room, and the man's clothing was worn, with

13

the bulge of a handgun showing under the raincoat. Perhaps she was one of those who'd come out here seeking a loved one. Still, the Irishman had the feeling it was more than that.

Crossing to a wide doorway, he went into the barroom and stepped to the oaken bar. The storm, he saw, had brought in others residing here, and some townspeople. Easing onto a stool at the front end of the bar, he ordered a hot brandy from the heavyset barkeep. "And another bottle of Four Roses."

"Shall I put it on your bill, Mr. O'Neal?"

"That'll be fine, Petey."

"Did you hear about the Salt Lake mail coach being held up?"

"Seems it isn't safe to travel anymore."

"Especially at night, Mr. O'Neal."

After the barkeep had placed his drink before him, Frank O'Neal studied through lidded eyes those clustered along the bar. Most of the tables were occupied, and the barroom was constructed so that open archways led into the spacious dining room finished in bluish tints. At a back table in the barroom a man wearing a sheriff's badge caught O'Neal's eye. Sheriff Henry Plummer was a suave, personable man about six feet in height. And according to rumors floating around Virginia City, Plummer could be mixed up with the highwaymen. The other man with him, O'Neal knew, was a sometime barrister named Sidney Clarkson, and just elected as mayor. Rotound, puffy of face, and with his black hair slicked down, Clarkson seemed to be directing the conversation. Whereas Plummer was clad in the clothing of an

14

outdoorsman, Sidney Clarkson had on a black frock coat over a black vest and string tie, and he had a full beard. The mayor had a big, pendulous lower lip like many men who talk a lot, mostly to hear their own voice.

O'Neal next studied a handsome, wavy-haired man seated alone in the dining room. He'd bucked George Banefield in an all-night poker game as had four others. Tucked away in a shoulder holster under the gambler's brown western-style coat was a five-shot American Pepper Box, a handy weapon up close, beyond twenty yards or so a person might as well be throwing rocks. Win or lose, Banefield always seemed to be flushed. Around here, Frank O'Neal had discovered, a man wasn't all he pretended to be, so perhaps the gambler was mixed up in crooked business.

Others whom O'Neal had gotten acquainted with were two drummers out of St. Louis, a local businessman residing here, some of the guests in evidence, and scattered throughout the barroom were a few miners garbed in rough clothing. Sipping at the hot brandy, O'Neal swung disinterested eyes at the mirrors strung along the back bar hewed out of cedar stained a dark brown. All of the lamps were hooded, while above the din of conversation could be heard the muted voice of the rainstorm. Then reflecting in one of the mirrors was the side door just to O'Neal's left being yanked open, and he glanced that way.

Steadying himself against the door stood highwayman Reno Lamont. His hat was gone, but the wounded man had no notion of that, or of his mud-splattered clothing. He stood swaying less than ten feet from Frank O'Neal, who wondered how a man so pale of face and with blood staining his clothes could still be alive. The hair plastered wetly to the highwayman's scalp and gaping eyes and grimacing of mouth as he tried to utter words stilled the conversation in the barroom, and then Reno Lamont pitched forward.

Immediately O'Neal slipped off the bar stool to step over the hardwood floor and kneel by the highwayman managing to swing over onto his back and gape up with eyes starting to dim, and O'Neal knew the man was only moments from death. Somehow Reno Lamont summoned enough strength to grab O'Neal's arm in a steely grip, and he gasped out in a whispery, straining voice, "It was . . . Ch . . . Chain . . . who done it!"

"I . . . can't hear you—"

"Still alive . . . Chain was—?" His hand fell away and death claimed the highwayman.

Now floorboards creaked as others moved ghoulishly to get a better glimpse of the dead man, and someone exclaimed, "Believe I've seen that man around town?"

"Seems I have too?"

"Did he say anything?"

Frank O'Neal suddenly realized those last words were directed at him, and coming erect, he looked into Sheriff Henry Plummer's inquiring dark brown eyes. "Nothing that made any sense. He must have been a foreigner."

"Yes," Henry Plummer murmured suspiciously, "we

have our share of them."

Then the former detective eased through those crowding for a better look at the body, picked up the full bottle of Four Roses, and slipped out of the barroom. Upstairs in his second-floor room, O'Neal poured a couple of fingers of the amber liquid into a glass and settled onto an overstuffed chair.

Frank O'Neal's first real job had been as an office boy for the Pinkerton Detective Agency, then he was allowed to do some investigative work, to leave after a year and learn more about his craft in Brooklyn, some months later to migrate over to Manhattan. He prided himself on his powers of deduction, the ability to read the character of those he came in contact with when working on a case and to pursue a lead regardless of where it took him. His weaknesses were a love of money and the nightlife one found in the vast confines of New York City. Later had come bouts with whiskey. He was a streetwise Irishman, not adverse to going after some ill-gained loot, but shying away from out-and-out thievery and murder.

"Now, O'Neal lad, that mon wot blundered into the barroom. It wasn't the shoulder or hip wound that done him in? And it appears he'd just come a considerable distance? So just to satisfy me curiousity I'll check out the stables come morning. Someone was waiting for him at the Commodore?"

And a sure instinct about these matters told O'Neal he hadn't seen the last of Sheriff Henry Plummer. Rising from the chair to the crackling of thunder, he drained the glass, placed it and the whiskey bottle on the dresser. Staring at his image in the mirror, the Irishman saw a man who could and would turn the dying words of highwayman Reno Lamont into monetary gain. A churlish smile tugging at his lips, he went over to make certain the door was locked. Undressing, he arranged his suit on a hanger, crawled under the covers and let the rainstorm lull him to sleep.

Across the street a shadow stirred in the dark yawning maw of an alleyway when the light flickered out in the Irishman's room. Then a match flared and flame was touched to a cigar to also light up the face of Sheriff Henry Plummer, who mutterd, "Why drag the Irishman into this?"

"We must know what Lamont said."

"Can't be all that damned important."

"If one watches his loose change, the dollars will take care of themselves."

"Yeah, I get your drift."

"If you want out, Henry, just say so—"

"Wanting out means I'll be signin my death warrant," he said bitterly. "Okay, okay, I'll palaver with O'Neal."

"I knew you would. By the way, some gold bullion will be shipped out with Peabody & Caldwell's stageline day after tomorrow."

"Where the hell do you get all your information?"

"I have my sources."

"Yeah, dammit, you sure as hell do!"

"Perhaps you want to know where the nightstalkers take those they kidnap—"

"No!" That word leaped out of Sheriff Plummer's

throat along with an upheaving of fear. He stood there as his companion hurried back down the alley. Suddenly the cigar didn't taste good, and he threw it away.

"Why," said a worried Henry Plummer, "did I get mixed up with that black devil?"

THREE

Frank O'Neal lingered over coffee in the dining room of the Commodore. An early riser, but for the local merchant who'd been in the barroom last night and two drummers holding an animated conversation about the hazards of traveling in these mountains, O'Neal sat alone with his thoughts. While shaving he'd nicked himself, a small cut at the point of his chin. Draped over his wiry frame was a brown vested suit, a matching derby catnapping on a chair to O'Neal's left. Angling through blue curtains came mellowy sunlight, telling the Irishman he wanted to leave before the morning crowd arrived. But the unexpected happening of last night caused O'Neal to refill his cup while glancing over at someone entering the dining room, a miner by his garb.

The anonymous security blanket he'd wrapped himself in had been stripped away all because of an empty bottle of Four Roses. Hard liquor, O'Neal's father as well as a succession of willing women had often told him, would be his downfall. He believed

21

otherwise, that his presence in the barroom was a lucky omen. It wasn't that he was withholding evidence from the sheriff, the dying words of the highwayman, since O'Neal felt that as a detective he'd been granted certain immunities from the law. Among these being the privilege of bribing witnesses, blackmail, the chance to turn a happening of this sort into a profit. This was the code of ethics Frank X. O'Neal lived by, and he enjoyed it. Through the pondering smile creasing his lips came the realization he'd grown tired of ambling from saloon to saloon, of swapping jokes or listening to the tired mutterings of men suddenly discovering that the only gold they'd find out here was in their teeth. Came the sobering notion also to O'Neal that he was buying chips in a dangerous game. This being determined to a great extent by the dark side of his Irish nature.

"So be it, lad," came his resigned words as a waitress appeared at his elbow.

"More coffee, Mr. O'Neal?"

"Ah, Molly dear, business calls me elsewhere." Clinking a silver dollar onto a saucer, he added, "And whatever brought you out to this heathen place?" More than once he'd found the eyes of Molly Carver upon him, a not unhandsome woman in her early thirties. The temptation was there to ask her out for a moonlight stroll, which could prove to be a dangerous venture in a place of sudden violence and death. She was the kind of woman men liked to confide in, and O'Neal couldn't help noticing that she received more tips than the other waitresses.

"My husband deserted me," she said bluntly. "Later I heard he died out in Colorado."

"I'm sorry to hear that."

22

"You needn't be."

Gesturing toward a chair, he said, "I wonder if you'll be interested in a little business venture—"

"If you're a carpetbagger, Mr. O'Neal, I barely earn enough to take care of my son." Somewhat reluctantly she sat down to his left.

"It's I who'll be wanting to pay you, Molly dear." He sipped at his coffee, and setting his cup down, cast her a guarded smile. "Last night a wounded man came into the barroom—he died in my arms, I might add."

"That's all we've been talking about this morning. They say it was Reno Lamont."

"Lamont?"

"That he could be a road agent."

"Judging from his appearance he traveled a considerable distance. Mere happenstance didn't fetch him to the Commodore."

"Did you notice anything peculiar," she whispered, "About his clothing?"

"I hadn't," confessed Frank O'Neal.

"Certain road agents wear black neckties fastened with a . . . a"—guardedly she gazed over O'Neal's shoulder at the kitchen door—"cordon knot."

"I do recall a necktie."

"It is the road agent's knot. They also identify one another by the peculiar way they shave down to a mustache and chin whiskers."

"Ay, Molly dear, this comes to mind."

"Are you connected with the law, Mr. O'Neal?"

"I'm just someone who wants justice done."

"Then you're in the wrong place."

"Indeed?"

"I understand Sheriff Plummer was there when that

23

man died."

"Along with our esteemed mayor."

"I trust neither man, especially the sheriff."

"Molly, I couldn't help noticing that those dining here seem to confide in you—"

"Just whatever it is you're seeking, Mr. O'Neal?"

"I really don't know. Just, I suppose, something that will tell me why that road agent came here." Reaching over, he pressed a double eagle into her hand. "There'll be more forthcoming, Molly, if you come up with something of importance."

Her steady eyes scanned his smiling face, and around a thoughtful smile of her own she murmured, "You did mention that road agent died in your arms, Mr. O'Neal. Which could mean that you were privy to his dying words?"

"Touché."

"That helping you could endanger my life."

"If you'd rather not?"

Molly Carver's grip tightened around the double eagle coin. "This is a lawless place. So I suppose somebody must take a stand, sooner or later. Anyway, the extra money'll come in hand."

"Just be your own sweet self, Molly dear, and things'll work out."

"Somehow I feel you're connected with the Federals—"

"My only interest, as I've stated, is to see justice done."

"Mr. O'Neal," she said cuttingly, "my demised husband was an Irishman. So cast all of this blarney aside."

Sweeping his derby off the chair as a trio of diners

came in to the room, O'Neal and the waitress rose together, and with the Irishman saying loudly, "Then it's agreed, Molly dear, we'll be going out for supper tomorrow night. Brisket of beef and sherry at the Virginia Hotel."

"Blarney, Frank O'Neal, seems to be your strong suit."

"Sevenish?"

"How can I resist your Gaelic charm?"

FOUR

Striding out from under the covered arcade in front of the Commodore Hotel, Frank O'Neal squinted away from dazzling shafts of sunlight pouring through a high gap in the distant Madisons. He ambled up the narrow street, the chill of night still there and edging under his coat while hoarfrost billowed out of his mouth, but the air he breathed was tangy fresh. His mood was one of wary eagerness now that he could put his past experience as a private investigator to good use again. While having the waitress Molly Carver help him was a stroke of luck, a commodity he'd seemed to have run out of lately. Around him Virginia City was awakening, and O'Neal would be willing to wager that before midmorning word would be carried into town of a body being found along one of the many trails or that someone was missing.

Coming to the east end of Cover Street and at its highest point, he stopped and turned to study Alder Gulch sweeping southerly as far as Summit City— north of Virginia City it downsloped past other mining

27

settlements, Nevada City, Pony, Alder, Highland, Adobetown. The source of water knifing along the gulch, the Stinking Water River, was lined from bank to bank with mining claims its entire length. Alder Gulch had been turned into a seventeen mile string of cabins, tents, dug-outs, caves or about anything that offered shelter to over ten thousand miners.

Now he glanced across the street at a man emerging from an alleyway and unlatching the front doors of a livery stable. Crossing over, O'Neal called out, "T'is a fine morning."

"In St. Louie, maybe," the hostler said acidly.

"A friend of mine borrowed my horse."

"Borrowed or stole's all the same to me."

"Told me he returned it last night."

"Not here he didn't 'cause we shutter up at sundown."

Flicking a couple of fingers at the brim of his hat, O'Neal sauntered away in search of another livery stable. He veered around some piney-scented two-by-fours stacked out in the street before clattering onto a boardwalk. Only to slacken his pace upon realizing he was passing by T.O. Smithson's Funeral Parlor. Rattling the brass knob, he found the door was locked, and quickly he cut along a side wall to the rear door, where he used a lock pick to gain access to the building. The dusty back room reeked of old blood and embalming fluids, but there on a wooden table lay the highwayman Reno Lamont. On the wide shelf of a nearby cabinet lay a few metal instruments of the undertaker's trade; tacked just above this to the log wall was a picture torn from a magazine of a bare-chested woman, the dead highwayman staring at the woman out of half-lidded eyes.

28

"She's not your type, Lamont," muttered O'Neal as he waved some flies away from the man's face.

The black necktie, as pointed out to him by Molly Carver, was held in place with a cordon knot, a mustache and chin whiskers adorning the highwayman's waxy contenance, and O'Neal came up with a few coins and some paper money and a rusty pocket knife in his search of the clothing. But there wasn't a shred of paper that contained the highwayman's identity or that could tell O'Neal of others who might be involved in these nefarious activities. He doubted, also, that anyone would claim the body.

The sound of a key rasping in the front door carried back to the Irishman. In his right hand he held almost two hundred dollars that belonged to the highwayman, and quickly he shoved twenty dollars, or the cost of a pine box, back into the man's pocket, then O'Neal scurried outside. Pausing in shadows flowing away from the back of the funeral parlor, he arranged the rest of the paper money in his thinning wallet, the few coins into his pocket.

"A nice windfall for the next game of chance," he murmured smugly, and with no twinge of scruples over taking the money.

Venturing back to Cover Street, he went down uneven stretches of boardwalk broken by short flights of steps or barren ground. Around him buggies and wagons rolled by, and locals and miners, and already most of the business places were doing a lively trade. Passengers were boarding a stagecoach out in front of the Wells Fargo & Co. office, the driver and shotgun chatting while taking their ease on the high front seat. Further along the street he bypassed the new glass-

29

fronted building of the *Montana Post,* remembering that its editor Thomas J. Dimsdale, one of the few intellectuals in the mining camps, had inquired over a glass of port wine just what had brought a private investigator out here. Needless to say, Frank O'Neal had avoided the man thereafter.

As he passed in front of the Nowlan & Weary Bank, the Irishman cast an apprehensive glance over his shoulder. For the notion had just come to him that someone could have been watching the funeral parlor; either one of Sheriff Plummer's deputies or the man the highwayman had come to see. And so he sauntered into Dance & Stuart's drygoods store and told the clerk, a scrawny man with a chalky face marred by pimpled skin, that he wanted a handful of those imported Havana cigars in that glass humidor.

"That'll be a buck and a quarter, mister."

"No problem," smiled O'Neal as he detached from his wallet some of the money just taken from the highwayman. "Are there any livery stables up this way?"

"Closest one is the OK Corral."

Nodding his thanks, he turned and moved to the open doorway, there to light one of the cigars while studying those moving by out on the street. Now it struck Frank O'Neal that he was being watched, and half turning, he stared back at a plump man of indeterminate age presiding over a shoe repair stand located along a side wall in the store. This, according to some bar talk he'd overheard, was an unsavory character named Clubfoot George. Under the shabby vest O'Neal's probing eyes could detect the outline of a small revolver. It was rumored that Clubfoot George was mixed up with some road agents, and one look at the man verified this in the Irishman's mind.

Outside, O'Neal angled to the southern side of the street, where he passed the Madison House and a couple of other stores before arriving at the OK Corral and livery barn. He paused to think while relighting his cigar; several horses were milling about in a pole corral and from their general appearance none of them had been ridden hard lately. He walked over to the livery barn, set back from the street with a large haystack shading its eastern wall. Dimly, beyond the open front doors, he could discern someone shoveling manure out of a runway passing down the middle of the dirt floor. Upon entering he found more horses tethered in the stalls.

"Morning," he said around the cigar.

The hostler merely glanced at the newcomer out of the corners of his eyes while bending to the task at hand. It was with a straining effort that he managed to dump another shovelful of manure into his wooden wheelbarrow. Under the shapeless felt hat and above the thick greying beard only his eyes and nose showed; his clothing was threadbare, and patched in places. He worked with a stoop to his shoulders, and slowly as the aged do.

"Mind if I look at that horse?" O'Neal said louder than he intended, only to have the hostler respond to his inquiry by fastening his grimy hands on the arms of the wheelbarrow and trundle it out the front door. Provoked by the man's silent treatment of him, O'Neal added testily, "Tightlipped as a banker."

On the upper railing of a stall occupied by a steel-grey bronc hung a worn saddle and a pair of saddlebags, both items still covered with caked mud. Edging alongside the horse, a closer examination of the saddle revealed to O'Neal blotches of blood. Unbuckling a saddlebag flap, he peered inside.

"That rigging belong to you?"

Startled, he glanced over at the hostler outlined in the back doorway. And staring down the barrel of a Deane-Adams. The stoop was gone from the man's shoulders, and as he stepped toward the stall with the easy grace of an outdoorsman, O'Neal suddenly realized he'd been hoodwinked, a thought which cut at his pride.

"To an acquaintance," he snapped.

"Reckon this means, Mr. O'Neal, you're mixed up with the nightstalkers!"

The morning grew ominously colder for Frank O'Neal when the hammer clicked back on the Deane-Adams, and he stammered, "That isn't the way of it, mister."

"You're from back east, New York; I'd hazard to say from . . . Brooklyn."

"I . . . I . . . yes—"

"Been in these parts about a month."

"Just . . . who are you?" Now sunlight streaming through a window back of O'Neal dusted the hostler's face. Somehow the greyish beard seemed to be some sort of disguise, one which couldn't conceal the youthful sparkle in those eyes. Also, there were some strange scars by the left eye. Even more alarming to the Irishman was how this man knew his name.

"Who I am is no concern at the moment, Mr. O'Neal. I trailed the rider of that horse in here."

"Obviously, then, you shot him," O'Neal found

himself saying.

His eyes narrowing bitterly, Ash Tamerlane said, "Just winged Reno Lamont. Now I won't be asking you again—are you one of them?"

O'Neal found himself backing against the stable wall and away from the murderous glint in the hostler's eyes. He knew his desire to pick up some easy money had backfired, would probably see him getting shot, and quickly he told of what had happened over at the Commodore Hotel. "That's it, mister. The Gospel truth, I swear."

"You've just confirmed what I've already found out," said Ash Tamerlane as he tucked the gun into his belt. "Seems you're just another opportunist. Well, so that highwayman said a man named Chain bushwacked him—"

"You're . . . Chain? Sure you are?"

"Reckon I be him, alright. I hear the sheriff is looking for you."

Although O'Neal carried in a shoulder holster a Colt New Line Pocket .41, there it would remain, for confronting him was a man of a caliber he'd never seen before. He doubted this Chain worked for the federal government, in any capacity. Or any territorial lawmen. It was possible the man was a bounty hunter. But somehow, the Irishman sensed, it cut deeper than that, and more in the shape of a personal vendetta.

"Figure him to be," he finally said. "Held out on Sheriff Plummer last night."

"Those who are behind the nightstalkers also hail from your old balliwick, Mr. O'Neal. Which darkens what I think about you being out here."

"I'm an honest tradesman—a private detective.

Business just happened to be slow back east. Anyway, the newspapers were full of what was going on out here."

A smile danced in Ash Tamerlane's eyes. "The bunco squad back in Manhattan would welcome the chance to find you."

Paling, O'Neal blurted out, "How did you find out about me?"

"Like you said, your eastern newspapers carry more than news about the discovery of gold out here. You should be thanking your lucky stars I didn't just up and kill you. Your demise would cause no ripple upon the conscience of this unlawful place. To get to the point, Mr. O'Neal, I need your help."

"As a detective, I'm assuming?"

"That, and your fullest cooperation—"

"Or?"

"A word in the wrong ears and someone else will cut you open."

"You, sir, are a hard man."

"Just one seeking revenge."

"I will receive a wage for my services," O'Neal questioned haughtily.

"Nothing!"

"Nothing?"

"A man of your rather dubious reputation had it in mind to gain some hard coin out of the highwayman's dying statement. Your mind-bent is only too clear to me, O'Neal."

"It seems you have me over the proverbial barrel. Or as Shakespeare would phrase it, 'It seems to me most strange that men should fear, Seeing that death, a necessary end—"

". . . Will end when it will come."

"So you're familiar with the works of the English bard too?"

"O'Neal, I want you to play the role of concerned citizen. Upon leaving here, I want you to head over to the sheriff's office and tell Plummer what that highwayman told you."

"But, wouldn't my telling Sheriff Plummer somehow endanger your life?"

"A risk I'll have to take. Think of it this way, O'Neal." Around a bittersweet smile he added, "Telling what you know just might save your own life."

Realizing that his own greed had trapped him, Frank O'Neal knew he had no choice but to do as this man wanted. And in Chain's voice there had been a certain timbre, of someone who'd been tested and not found wanting. What quickened the pounding of his heart now was also the realization that Chain was pitting himself against some very bloodthirsty men. So the choice was his, O'Neal knew, to die at the hand of this man or others. That he was frightened revealed itself when he spoke in a quivering voice.

"Where can I find you?"

"I'll find you."

Then, Ash Tamerlane was gone, and the Irishman muttered bitterly, "I've no doubt you will, lad, none a-tall!"

FIVE

Ash Tamerlane meandered down side streets and vacant lots until he reached the lower end of Wallace Street and the Picard boarding house. Easing through a side door, he took a rickity flight of stairs to his small room on the second floor. Locking the door behind him, he dropped his hat on the iron cot and stood before a curtained window. Wearily he rubbed the side of his neck while surveying Virginia City sweeping eastward toward the cloud-scudded sky.

The citizenry of the Fairweather Mining District, of which Virginia City was a part, seemed to be gripped in a malaise of fear caused by a lawless breed of cutthroats and thiefs. It was the same old pattern repeating itself as had been the case in other mining areas. Sooner or later honest men would take matters into their own hands, but this was of little concern to Tamerlane. In and around Alder Gulch the bloodthirsty hand of the Cartel had revealed itself.

On his list of suspects appeared the name of Sheriff Henry Plummer, a con man of the first order.

Tamerlane also knew that Plummer's deputies had paper out on them. It was easy to see how a scoundrel with Henry Plummer's charm could get elected to the office of sheriff. Sidney Clarkson, Virginia City's rather inept mayor, preferred going about politiking rather than keeping his sheriff in line. Matters were coming to a head though, since he'd heard rumors some of the businessmen were going to form a vigilante committee. These were just a couple of minor characters in this unfolding plot of sudden death and thievery. Somewhere in Virginia City was the front man of the Cartel, a conscienceless sort dispensing orders to the nightstalkers. Tamerlane hadn't overlooked the possibility this person could be a woman; a ploy used by the Cartel in the past.

Now the streets of Virginia City dimmed away as into Ash Tamerlane's eyes appeared the unfocused look of a man suddenly confronted with his own past, and destiny. Turning away from the window, Tamerlane stepped to the dresser and removed the false beard, then stared bitterly at his image reflected in the mirror. He saw the face of a man just turned thirty. There'd been no need to tint hair turning prematurely grey. Testifying to the hard life he'd led over the past decade were the deep lines cutting harshly into his weathered skin; the scar there bearing further testimony to sudden violence, and always reminding him of those he meant to kill. Reaching for the bottle of corn liquor, the western aqua vitae, he poured some liquor into a glass before lifting a tintype out of his makeup kit, one of the legacies left him by his actor father. Opening the tintype, Tamerlane gazed wistfully at a picture of his family.

Downing the contents of the glass, he let himself drift deeper into days of yore and back to New York City where his father had performed on Broadway, having his name on marquees alongside others such as Lotta Crabtree, David Belasco, Edwin Boothe. John Tamerlane had been a master of disguise and of mimicry, and with equal ease the actor could play roles in Shakespeare as well as Gilbert and Sullivan's The Mikado, skills he passed on to his son, Ash. There'd been ocean voyages to Europe, and acting roles in London and Paris, along with one memorable journey on the Orient Express, to detour down through Italy and board a ship for Cairo. A safari into Darkest Africa had found Ash Tamerlane, at age 17, downing a charging rhino and killing other big game.

Upon returning to New York and the glittering lights along Broadway, John Tamerlane found himself returning home one day to tell his family he'd invested in a western mining venture. "Out Colorado way," he exulted. And then for a change of pace, the actor packed bag and baggage and family aboard a train to play the river towns—Nashville, Cincinnati, Natchez, to finally wind up at New Orlean's St. Philip Street Theater.

"Well, my dear husband, here's another telegram from your investors."

A smiling John Tamerlane turned to embrace his wife in the privacy of his dressing room while gazing fondly at his children, Ash and Melanie. After kissing his wife, he scanned the brief contents of the wire, murmured worriedly, "Seems they want more money."

"Who are these people, John?"

"Now, dear," he told his wife, "let's not concern

ourself with money matters."

"But I must, John. Your son will be a junior at Harvard this fall."

"Have I ever failed you before? Besides, these men I'm involved with . . . and I might add, dear, some very influential people back in Manhattan, have assured me the few thousand I invest with them will make us independently wealthy. Then the only acting I'll be doing is at a high stakes poker game. We're heading for Colorado."

"Colorado?"

"Dear wife, that's where the gold mine is. Just want to check out what I've gotten myself into."

"This'll be great," said Ash. "It wasn't my idea to become a lawyer."

Immediately thereafter the Tamerlanes were enroute for western Colorado. Upon arriving at Placerville strung along the Dolores River, John Tamerlane's inquiries about a gold mine owned by the United Investment Company brought only a silent shaking of heads. Worried now, he went to other frontier towns in the Paradox Valley, to finally learn of one mine that was located someplace amidst a rugged barrier of rocks and ravines called the Uncompahgre Plateau. The sheriff of Redvale told the actor his life could be in danger, to take his family back east. But the warning came too late, as in the darkness of night armed men broke into the Tamerlane's rooms in a local hotel and used their long knives to silence everyone except the son, Ash Tamerlane, whom they brought struggling and chained to their mountainous hide-out.

Just turned 20, Ash came to know the agonizing bite of whips and lengths of chain. Existing on a meager

40

diet of cornbread and beans and spring water, the hatred came as his body leaned, then began to sicken. Daily he toiled away with either pick or shovel in the underground mine. He came to dread those lashing chains that could kill or disfigure, which was his fate after incurring the wrath of hulking nightstalker Reno Lamont. To Ash and the others the sun was an unseen, alien star, for they labored long hours under lanterns and rested by moonlight, that in a stockade and on barren ground, and with their roof a canopy of uncaring stars.

"I'm dying—"

It took a moment for those words to make sense to Ash Tamerlane on the deep edge of sleep. Blinking his eyes open, he turned that way and clutched the shoulder of a luckless cowpoke named Red. "Hang in there," he said desperately, "there's got to be a way out of here."

"Not . . . not for me, Ash. Listen . . . pard, over-heard them nightstalkers talking on . . . on killing us off—"

"They need us."

"Needed us . . . you mean. The ore's thinning out." He sought to draw air into his lungs while in the sunken hollows of his skully face the cowpoke's eyes were beginning to dim. "Get away, Ash . . . tonight." The next moment he was dead.

The following evening, and seemingly in answer to Ash Tamerlane's prayers, a rainstorm struck the plateau. Despite being hindered by the ankle irons, Ash managed to get out of the stockade hewed out of rocks and piney logs and make his way up a rain-slicked, bouldered wall to an escarpment. Slumping down, he wiped rainwater away from his face with a clay-streaked hand. The climb had exhausted Ash, the hampering leg irons sapping his strength. Though the cold driving rain had soaked his tattered clothing, it had also driven most of the guards to cover. By his reckonings, the cliff he was on ran due west into country unknown to him. He'd have to beeline south for the Paradox Valley, which, he recollected, was a good three days ride. Striking on foot for the valley would take him at least a week, and without any food, he knew his chances of getting there were slim.

Summoning what energy he had left, Ash lurched to his feet just as spearing a glaring track across the inky sky came lightning to outline him to the disbelieving eyes of his captors.

"Hey! Up there!"

"Get him!"

Through a ragged volley of riflefire Ash stumbled backwards to scramble upward on the sloping face of the cliff. As leaden slugs chipped rock fragments around him, he gained rimrock and dove out of sight. Gasping, he suddenly realized pieces of granite dislodged by the bullets had embedded into his arms and torso. Ignoring the pain, he came erect and plunged forward blindly, pushed by fear, the grim knowledge they'd soon be after him. He slammed into the spreading branches of a limber pine, staggered sideways, but kept on the move despite the blinding darkness gripping the rimscape. Then, was it his scream that ricocheted away or the clashing thunder, for Ash found himself stepping off into air, then cartwheeling and plummeting downward. He struck a shelf of sloping rock, cried out in pain, the force of

42

his fall carrying him away, and once again when he struck something solid he felt no more.

The awful memory of what had transpired that night returned from time to time to haunt Ash Tamerlane. Later, after his captors had given him up for dead, Ash descended to a draw while favoring a broken left arm and followed it southward under a new day's sun. Two days passed before a couple of prospectors guided by circling vultures came upon young Tamerlane crawling toward the enticing waters of a spring. Loading him aboard a pack mule, they fetched him along to their high plateau claim where Ash slowly regained his health.

"Yup, Ash," one of the miners revealed one day, "I've heard of that hell-hole you was took to."

The other prospector said, "A heap of folks including some friends of ours have disappeared sudden-like."

"These people murdered my family," said Ash. "The men behind this are some eastern investors."

"Got any inkling who they are, son?"

"I'll find out—then kill the lot of them!"

And after leaving the prospectors, Ash Tamerlane returned to the Paradox Valley and visited the gravesite of his family. Afterwards he wandered through valley towns searching for men who might have ridden with the nightstalkers. Only to learn from a U.S. marshal that the gold mine he'd been held captive at had been abandoned. Thus began a decade-long search, of Ash heading down to Texas and hiring on as a cowpuncher at various ranches and of trying his hand at gambling. From there he ventured northward to new mining towns springing up along the spiny mountain ranges, a trail which finally brought him at the age of 30 here to Virginia City. Along the way he'd picked up various names, the modus operandi of the Cartel, the chilling realization there'd be no more trails after this. He was bone-weary, embittered, hard of heart and mind.

SIX

In the guise of a cattle buyer Ash Tamerlane left the boarding house and struck out for uptown Virginia City. Settled rakishly on his head was a dark brown cattleman's hat; the light brown coat with elbow patches hung open showing a leather vest and string tie, the seamed trousers riding down over handtooled boots. A few touches of hair dye had darkened Ash's side-burns and mustache. His stride was brisk, with his eyes alert to the morning activity.

Distantly one of those lonesome cloud banks with a fat black underbelly had intentions of dumping rain upon city limits within the hour—other cloud formations were rising along the southern and western quarters of the mellow-blue sky. The mountain range rose around him, sometimes stippled with forest, more often sheer rock pinnacles. The discovery of gold had changed the gulch from a pleasant summering spot to a place of greed and death, mused Tamerlane. There was the stench of danger, a feeling strong in him that one mistake on his part would be his last. But he welcomed what was to come.

Upon reaching Wallace Street, Ash slowed down and reached for the makings. While shaping a cigarette, he eyed about twenty freight wagons being pulled by mules coming into line before a mercantile store. Striding amongst the wagons and bellowing orders to muleskinners went a man Tamerlane had bested at poker a couple of nights ago, burly, red-haired Irish Joe Finney, who was no great shakes as a player but didn't fret when he lost. Finney's was a dangerous profession, since the road agents seemed to know when a wagon train was carrying gold bullion. Even though wagonmaster Finney had handpicked most of his men, this was never an assurance one of them couldn't be working with the outlaws. This train would head down into the Gallatin Valley and go over to Red Lodge for supplies.

And by now, Tamerlane pondered as he moved on, Frank O'Neal should have talked to Sheriff Henry Plummer, who'd have passed this information on to the Cartel's front man. As for O'Neal, the man was nothing more than a fast-buck artist—a sort not to be trusted. But Ash realized he had little choice in the matter, since he needed someone to keep an eye on things here in Virginia City while he tried to find that hidden gold mine. O'Neal's background as a detective should stand him in good stead, that is, if he didn't let his greed overrule his common sense.

Daily more people flooded in, both honest and crooked men, who lost little time in joining an outlaw gang. So it was difficult for Tamerlane to fit a face to a name, meaning he'd have to keep a closer eye on Plummer and his deputies, Ned Ray and Buck Stinson, and be ready to follow them when they left the city. It wasn't clear yet to Tamerlane whether Plummer was actually involved in any robberies, though it was plain the man was connected to the nightstalkers.

Before going into Coleman & Loeb's Saloon, Tamerlane gazed at Irish Joe Finney's freight wagons rolling to the east. Any gold bullion would be scattered among the wagons. They were experienced mule-skinners, heavily armed, and with several outriders, the odds in favor of their getting through. Briefly he thought about saddling his horse and trailing after the wagons. It was just past nooning, which meant the freight wagons would be coming off the Tobacco Roots around nightfall. Finney and his men could hold off an army, he finally decided, and turned and shouldered through the batwings.

Coleman & Loeb's was just another square-framed building with its high-ceilinged interior divided into the front barroom to where a walled partition screened off most of the gaming tables. There were no bar girls, just three barkeeps passing out glasses of foamy beer and bottles of whiskey, a place a shade tamer than the others. Bypassing the long, crowded bar, Tamerlane drew up to watch a roulette wheel spin to a stop, the gambler running it smiling out of his eyes when the bouncing pellet landed on the red to spell losers for the three players.

"Alright, gents," he intoned callously, "place your bets."

"You sure this is an honest wheel?"

"I'm a Quaker, Jake," smiled the gambler.

"And this Iscariot fella was one of the apostles. Ten more on the red."

"Well, Mr. Benning. How's the cattle business?"

Glancing at the gambler, Ash Tamerlane said, "Expecting a herd from Texas most any day now. Should bring a fair price here."

"I peg you as being from . . . San Antonio—"

"Thereabouts," drawled Tamerlane as he ambled away. In this and other Virginia City bars and gambling casinos he was known as Jim Benning, an easygoing gent and ready with a smile or to buy a round. He'd picked up a lot of bar talk, discarded most of it. Amid the chatter at the games had been an undertone of fear, the talk guarded, for none of the players wanted to draw attention to himself in a place where a casual acquaintance could be an outlaw.

When one of the players swung up and left the poker table, Tamerlane stepped that way and said softly, "Mind if I set in?"

"Long's you got money," responded a miner with pimples and the expression of a loser on his grimy face.

Fishing his wallet out of an inner coat pocket, Tamerlane fingered out some paper money. He sat down and looked at a man decked out in a rumpled black suit, a rug dealer out of Wichita, he recalled. "Seeing as how you're big winner in this game, how's about selling me a few chips?"

"How much?"

"Couple of hundred."

"Recollect you to be that cattle buyer," said the carpetbagger as he passed to Tamerlane a fistful of red and black chips.

Tamerlane settled into the game, but played cautiously as he caught snatches of conversation drifting over from other tables. Onlookers came and went, and sunlight no longer struck into eastern windows when he cashed in his chips and headed for another saloon. One of those gaudy calendars handed out by a brewery salesman was pinned to the back bar next to a row of liquor bottles of various shapes and sizes. The stein of beer he'd ordered came sliding across the varnished bar top. Hooking an unspurred boot on the brass railing, out of habit he brushed the flap of his coat away from the butt of his Deane-Adams before glancing about for signs of men having beards or bandanas like that which had adorned nightstalker Reno Lamont.

"Seems you're a stranger out here too."

Turning that way, he said, "Reckon so."

"Name's Fridley . . . Jason Fridley. Been trying to hire some carpenters to put up a store. Seems wages aren't cheap out here."

"But life is," said Tamerlane.

"You must be a cowboy?"

"Was once upon a lonesome time." Around a tightlipped smile Ash Tamerlane left the bar and his untouched drink.

Out on Cover Street, he grimaced up at that cloud bank he'd seen earlier just fringing upon city limits, a cold wind tugging at him along with wind-flung rain splatters, and he began crossing the street. Horsemen and carriages went by, and lumber wagons to disgorge their loads of raw timber and boards at building sites. A little over a month ago Tamerlane had first set eyes upon Alder Gulch and its boomtowns, realized that it wouldn't be too long before Virginia City would run out of usable land. And some would make it big, while others would either perish or leave.

Coming out of the Virginia Hotel was a bonneted,

darkhaired woman who returned his inquiring stare, and for the briefest of moments it was as if Wyomia Culver had entered his life again. Wyomia had been his first love. With that flush of remembrance came thoughts of how it had been at Harvard, now an alien world so far removed from this rugged place. A classmate had dragged Ash to a formal ball put on by one of the fraternities, where he'd endured a few dances with plumpish debutantes looking for eligible husbands, and then on the verge of leaving, he could still remember quite distinctly a clock chiming somewhere in the ballroom as he turned toward the main entrance to find her just entering, Wyomia. Through the swirling dancers their eyes had seemed to seek one another, and it was as if both of them had said, "Ah, there's the one!" By common accord they found each other among the press of couples dancing to the strains of a waltz by Mozart, came together and lost themselves in the music and an unspoken awe. For the remainder of that college year they were inseparable, friends, lovers, and with romantic notions of getting married. Suddenly, just before summer break, they'd quarreled, with Ash leaving to accompany his family on that ill-fated trip to New Orleans and westward. That had been over ten years ago, Ash told himself, as rainwater started pelting the street; and Wyomia, after learning of his demise, would have found another.

Grimacing, Ash tugged at his hat and hurried across the pebbled and debris-littered street and found the Anaconda Saloon, as did others. He sidled up to the bar next to a threesome of miners complaining about being overcharged in local stores, and with one of them sort of throwing in that he'd just acquired a social disease. Hooking an unspurred boot on the railing, Tamerlane glanced around the crowded saloon and beyond to one of the back tables just as one of the poker players tossed in his hand. George Banefield seemed to have a lot of connections around Virginia City—and the gambler had been there the night Reno Lamont had come dying into the Commodore Hotel.

"Howdy, Mr. Benning," said the barkeep, and setting a stein of beer down. "I hear some cattle'll be coming in any day now."

"Out of Texas." He clinked a silver dollar down next to the glass and nodded to his left. "Seems that gambler pays out more than he takes in."

"Banefield? Man's awful careless about how he bets."

"Unless he's betting that way a'purpose."

"You mean not givin' a hoot?"

"Obviously somebody's bankrolling the gambler."

"You know, Mr. Benning, that just could be." The barkeep leaned closer to add in a guarded whisper, "Seen that gambler chumming around with the sheriff. It was the same night Reno Lamont died. Me, I was right here a bar-keepin' until . . . I'd say around ten o'clock. Took off because this rainy weather was sure a'playin Hades with my rheumatism. I was sort'a beelining over to my rooming house, that's Mrs. Stewart's place, when I chanced to spot these two men lurkin' in an alley just north of the Commodore. A closer look showed them to be Sheriff Plummer and Banefield here. Couldn't hear much, but when it lightning I sure enough got a good look at Plummer's face . . . plumb scared, he were."

"Interesting? Did you hear anything at all?"

"I figured at the time, Mr. Benning, eavesdroppin' might prove injurious to my health. But it sure makes a person wonder—"

"Obliged," murmured Tamerlane as he passed to the barkeep a couple of silver dollars.

"Refill?"

"One's about my limit."

"Why this interest in Banefield?"

"Like you said before, he's mighty careless with his money. Could be Banefield is working with some outlaws. And sure hate to have that herd rustled."

"Speaking of outlaws and such, about a half-hour ago I spotted some of Sheriff Plummer's deputies riding out. Southeast, it appears."

With a nod for the barkeep, a former miner, Tamerlane left the saloon and went downstreet hurriedly. It was possible gambler Banefield was blackmailing Sheriff Plummer. Or that both men worked for the Cartel, and with Banefield as its paymaster. Recalling how the Cartel had operated down in Colorado, he knew that Banefield would be taking orders from someone else—a mine owner perhaps, some businessman, or public figure.

But his immediate concern was to follow those deputies. They could be on their way to tell a gang of road agents another wagon train had left Alder Gulch bound for Red Lodge. It was clearing by the time he reached the livery stable, threw rigging on his horse and rode out of town. Crossing a shallow fork of the Stinking Water, he came across shod-tracks of two loping horses. But as late afternoon dimmed away he lost them. The trail he'd followed had brought Tamerlane veering southerly along the high reaches of

52

the Tobacco Roots.

Reining up, he said, "No sense riding into an ambush."

And he swung his horse sideways and gazed at dusk closing rapidly upon the valley called Gallatin laying eastward. Someplace on its wide expanse Irish Joe Finney and his muleskinners would be circling their wagons for the night.

Then, upward Ash Tamerlane's worried eyes went to the moon poking over the horizon, a full moon, a killer's moon.

SEVEN

"I don't like it!"

"The moon?"

Around a baleful glare at the muleskinner, Irish Joe Finney hawked tobacco juice at the ground. "That among other things. Seems too peaceful out here . . . for my liking."

"Don't reckon, Joe, anybody would be foolhardy enough to attack a train of our size."

"My aching bones tell me contrarywise. How many men are standing guard?"

"Three right now; they'll be spelled within the hour."

"Roust Murdock and that other scout out of their bedrolls and have them saddle up."

"Heck, all they'll scare up out here is some jackrabbits, a coyote or two. I tell you, Joe, it's too cantankerous bright out for any highwaymen to hit us tonight."

"Tend to it!" barked Finney as he shouldered around and strode out through an opening between two wagons. Stirring in his belly was a gripping unease so strong it caused bile to rise in his throat. Here they were, out on the valley floor with no shelter to speak of, just the few trees by this creek and a cut-bank rising maybe ten feet, and the wagons.

In the last two or three hot summer months, his thoughts rambled on, a lot of men had gone under at the hands of those murdering road agents. And these cutthroats were getting bolder, hitting in broad daylight now, then brazenly spending their ill-begotten gains at the mining towns abounding in Alder Gulch. And striking at night, always at night, were a new breed called the nightstalkers. Rarely did a man come back to tell of their forays, but Irish Joe Finney had had conversation with such a person, a Finlander named Okeson, who told of pretending to be dead after being plugged at close range with a scatter-gun, laid there as those of his comrades who survived were chained aboard their horses and taken away. As his teeth clamped down on the plug of chewing tobacco and tore a hunk away, a sense of dread gripped Finney.

"What in the name of all that was Holy," he questioned, "would these grave robbers be doing with these men? Or taking them?" Back in Ireland there'd been whispered tales of vampires and werewolfs and such. "But this was Montana. In God's name what's happening?" Came a cold wind rustling through prairie grass to find Irish Joe Finney, and he shuddered inwardly. Now the soft clop-clop of shod hoofs told him his scouts were heading out.

The scouts, after leaving the wagon train, followed their backtrail to the gravelly track running down into the Gallatin Valley. One of them, Murdock by name, was a seasoned Indian scout, and he told his companion, "Seems out of sorts Finney acting like this—"

"Irishmen have their black moods."

"So do the Sioux, Crow."

"Well, Murdock, you're the expert in these matters. What now?"

"We earn our pay," he said laconically. Ike Murdock, burly, with a thick blackish beard resting upon his broad chest, wore mocassins and a fringed leather suit and beaver cap; he appeared to be in his late forties. Through a wondering glimmer dancing in his pale eyes he studied the dark hulk of the Tobacco Roots cloaked in moonlight. Perhaps it was a worry he shared with Finney, or a honed instinct that had kept him alive all these dangerous years; in any case, scout Ike Murdock sensed a presence. There were Indians, Bannacks, the vengeful Blackfeet; further east the Crow and Arikara Sioux. A man could get spooked at all that had happened in these parts lately. Sometimes he felt the Indian had more civilized ways than these Johnny-come-lately white men who despoiled the virgin territory with their greed. Calmly now, he let his senses take command of the situation, keening his ears to the familiar night sounds as his nostrils probed the air for that smoky aroma of the Indian, an odor caused by the smoke of their fires and the furry, wild-tanned leather they wore.

"Well?"

"It ain't Injun out there," Murdock finally concluded.

"So we head back?"

"Nope." Impatiently he eyeballed his companion. "Something's amiss."

"Road agents?"

"It sure in tarnation ain't polar bears. There's two or three known routes out of them mountains, a few game trails. Meanin' I don't think they followed us down this pass. By the moon it's shyin' onto midnight. So's with any luck we'll spot what's left of their campfire."

"If they made any," the other muttered skeptically. But he'd voiced it to the near darkness for Ike Murdock had ghosted away, and the scout clucked his grey the opposite way, north and upward to follow among shrubbery and trees growing in the canyon.

As the scout passed warily amongst a copse of aspens set to shivering by a slight wind, there came to him a whispering sound as of a night bird of prey passing on beating wings. Only to have that feathery noise expire when an arrow pierced deep into his chest. The scout dropped silently to the mossy ground and tried to drag himself toward a nearby boulder, before there came looming over him a dark shape, the blade of the knife he clutched slicing the scout's throat from corner to corner.

In the time remaining to Ike Murdock, scouting further south, penetrating his mind came a grim awareness that near at hand someone had just died. Instantly he swung to the ground, alarming his horse so that it whickered as he unsheathed his Springfield rifle. He crouched away from the horse and under a limber pine while sensing a dangerous presence closing upon him. Death came in the shape of an arrow shafting into his exposed back and servering his spinal cord.

A dark-clothed man, but not the one who'd killed Ike Murdock, darted up to the body. Toeing it over, he called out, "He's dead."

58

"Remove his clothes and put them on," came a disembodied voice. "You, and you, catch his horse."

The moon was higher now, almost midnighting over the wagons where Irish Joe Finney waited anxiously for his scouts to return. Much to his relief the wind had died down, so that any alien sound could be picked up. Except for three men standing guard and Finney's foreman lurking to his right, the other outriders and muleskinners were wrapped in their bedrolls. The livestock was penned within the encircled wagons. Rapping an impatient knuckle against the wagon box, Finney rasped, "How long they been out there?"

"Going on two hours."

"Long time to be chasing shadows, I reckon."

"Don't worry, Joe, if there's anything out yonder Murdock'll find it, be they whites or Injuns."

Though the temptation was strong in Finney to wake up the others, he knew his men needed their rest. All summer they'd been making that long, arduous trek to Red Lodge for supplies that could carry Virginia City through the wintry months. Enroute they had passed burned out wagons or the bloated remains of oxen and mule or horse, and grave markers, generally a pile of stones or a wooden cross. While up along Alder Gulch there'd been talk of forming a vigilante committee. But that's all it was, just talk among the merchants and miners—meanwhile the highwaymen went about their killing business. Despite the return of his scouts, Finney still couldn't calm down, and when some of the mules started milling and braying again, a worried oath

59

passed through his taut lips.

Then, before Irish Joe Finney's startled eyes, both scouts swerved their horses at an angled gallop which carried them away from the wagons. And even as Finney shouted a warning, seemingly out of nowhere black-clad marauders were dashing in on foot between the wagons. A shot rang out, the guard who'd fired it cut down in a vicious crossfire. Those who'd been sleeping leaped up from their bedrolls to find themselves surrounded by armed men, while a rifle prodding Finney in the back caused him to drop his weapon.

"Surrender or die!"

"Do what they say!" Finney shouted to some of his men still grasping their weapons.

And suddenly it was over, with the marauders disarming Finney's men, and with others bringing in their horses. Quickly a search of the wagons produced all of Finney's gold bullion, leaving the wagonmaster with the grim knowledge one of his men had sold him out. Now by torchlight chains were wrapped around the upper bodies of those who'd been captured, and their wrists manacled before they were hoisted aboard the mules.

"Hey," a muleskinner exclaimed, "I know you?"

Blue flame erupted from the marauder's gun barrel with the slug gouging out the muleskinner's right eye, and he fell dead to the ground. Holstering his handgun, the marauder reached for one of the torches. With the yellowish flame flickering over him, he moved to stand facing Finney's men, and there to say grimly, "I be Boone Helm!" Large, with thickcorded neck muscles, Helm was clad entirely in black. He had chin whiskers and a wide face revealing his cruel nature. Thick black brows lay above icy green eyes devoid of any human spark, and his voice had been gutteral and deep-pitched. Slowly there issued from his mouth a mocking laugh as of creek water flowing over a pebbled bottom, the laughter coming harsher now to lash out at the frightened men he'd just captured. Helm's green eyes never lidded, the expression on his face one of pure hatred.

"We," he went on, "are the nightstalkers!"

"No!" one of the muleskinners cried out. "Not that!" Somehow he kneed the mule he sat on into motion, a futile effort, for there came hissing through the moonlight a length of chain that coiled itself around the man's neck, a hard tug from the man grasping its other end spilling the muleskinner to the ground.

"Is he still alive?" inquired Boone Helm.

"Neck's broken."

"A pity," said Helm through mirthless laughter. "Let's move out." Wheeling around, he threw the torch into a wagon bed.

"Please . . . please," called out Irish Joe Finney, "where are you taking us? We . . . we have a right to know—"

"To a place where you'll never see sunlight again!"

Steadily, cautiously, Ash Tamerlane brought his horse toward the burning wagons. It was that quiet hour before dawn, the light still uncertain, the night birds of prey making one last sweep before seeking their nests. Dew clung to prairie grass while a mist floated along the creek bottom Tamerlane was approaching. His sheepskin helped ward off the chill, but any discomforts were forgotten when he glimpsed amongst the burning wagons a couple of dead men.

Turning his horse, he eased just outside the burning wagons while scanning the strewn ground for the trail taken by the nightstalkers. Upon finding it, he rode over to the creek. He left his horse there and ventured among the charred remains of the wagons until he came up with a shovel. He dug graves for the murdered men on a high bank overlooking the creek, and then buried them. Next he fashioned a campfire, and when it was ready, slowly ate a breakfast of chicory coffee, bacon and sourdough biscuits. Hunkered there still over a second cup of coffee, he knew that any haste on his part to head out after the nightstalkers would be foolhardy.

The trail left by these evil men went due north. Later today, he reasoned, they would bring their prisoners up into the Tobacco Roots. He'd scouted the middle range of these mountains before, failed to locate their mine. However, there were still a lot of undiscovered gold and silver lodes up there, as well as in other mountain ranges. And it simply wasn't a matter of tracking the nightstalkers, since they were a canny lot, keeping watch on their backtrail, and perhaps holding their captives at some hidden place for a few days before bringing them to the gold mine. Theirs was a well-conceived organization, backed by the brains and money of the Cartel, a sinister group of men to whom time meant nothing, wealth everything, and the crucible by which they measured their success.

Lingering until the sun had cleared the peaks of the Madisons to the east, Tamerlane picked up the trail of the nightstalkers and followed it northward. He spurred his horse into a lope, knowing from the low position of the sun its blinding rays would conceal him from the searching eyes of those he pursued.

"When will this end?"

That question slipped unbidden into his mind. Somehow it seemed he'd been after these men most of his life. Yet, the fires of vengence burned brighter than ever, with no thought on Ash Tamerlane's part as to what his future held. For the future was this moment, in the tracks he followed, the promise his Deane-Adams or Winchester would down some of the nightstalkers before the sun tracked its way over the western horizon again.

EIGHT

They were good, Tamerlane mused with dark admiration, keeping up their pace this way, as he followed hoofprints dusting a rising canyon in the Tobacco Roots. Shadows were etching on the loamy ground shapes of trees and large boulders, and it was cooling with night's approach. Only once had the nightstalkers taken a breather, that around mid-afternoon and just before heading into this canyon, to leave behind a few charred cigarette butts and an empty whiskey bottle, the drying stools of their mounts. To get this far they'd ridden hard, which could only mean the nightstalkers had some fresh mounts waiting up on the mountain. It occurred to Ash they could have spotted him, a chance he'd have to take. And if they had, they would probably figure him for just another hardcase wanting to hook in with a wild bunch. Besides, one gun wasn't much of a threat to a couple of dozen armed men.

A creek murmuring off to Tamerlane's left brought him over there, and tiredly he swung to the ground and let his horse drink. This was a bronc, a rangy bay he'd paid hard cash for over in Nevada, and which had a mulish way of doing things. Its previous owner had given up any notions of turning it into a cutting horse, sold it to Tamerlane shy of market price. Between them had sprung up an uneasy truce, the bronc still skittish and wanting to buck, the man who'd bought it keeping a tight rein on his patience, simply because the bronc had more than average stamina and a good bottom, had proven to be surefooted in high plateau country.

After slaking his thirst and refilling his canteen, Ash took out an old pair of field glasses and checked out the upper reaches of the canyon. The only movement detectable were a few birds flitting about and what turned out to be a whitetail grazing across a small clearing before vanishing among thick shrubbery. In him was the urge to move on—wait until nightfall, he cautioned himself. Another few hours weren't important, or days. Out of a saddlebag he removed some beef jerky; easing down on a patch of grass he smiled thinly at the bronc nibbling at some wild flowers.

When first starting after those who'd murdered his family, Tamerlane had been so consumed by hatred that he hadn't minded lonely campsites, not having others around to jaw with over a cold meal. He pondered, as night edged closer, how these seeking years had changed his notions of what was right or wrong, or even proper. Once in a while there'd been a wayward woman, either a dance hall girl or harlot to share his bed. At first he'd felt some guilt, but that had dimmed out too, along with that picture of Wyomia he carried around in his thoughts. He'd acquired the skills of shooting and tracking, and horsemanship while

66

employed as a cowpuncher, realized the Great Plains and mountains had become a place of great beauty and solitude he could never leave; liquor had played a role, too, as had gambling.

Rising, he strode over to his grazing horse only to have it bare its teeth and sidle away. "I hear back east, hoss, there's a glue factory in need of horsemeat." Grasping the ground-hitched reins, he climbed into the saddle, and with the bronc snorting its displeasure but obeying a jab to head out from Ash's spur.

Right off he discovered there was no discernible track to follow up the canyon. And with night settled in, the climb would be hazardous. So he let the bronc have its head, and after a while it found a game trail laboring and twisting around trees and rocky ground. Every so often he drew rein to check out the lay of the higher ground, or for any noise that might carry down or the flare of a campfire. From the eastern horizon to overhead, huge glittering star formations helped to light Tamerlane's passage, the mountain wall blocking his view of stars to the west. When the pitch steepened, Ash slid to the ground and went ahead of his horse. Oftentimes his boots would slip out from under him, and then, as the moon rose to mock his efforts, he stepped onto the plateau stippled with Douglas firs and lesser trees.

Quickly he brought his horse away from the ribbon of trail and into the pine forest of the mountain. When the bronc settled in to grazing at the sparse grass growing under the trees, he knew the nightstalkers had kept on the move. In the saddle again, he rode deeper into the mountain, skirting the edges of clearings and drawing up at rocky ledges to scan the vast open ground beyond for any sign of a campfire. After a while the moon came ghosting overhead, and by this time Tamerlane realized the nightstalkers had no idea he'd been following them, that they'd be bedded down. And not wanting to chance stumbling onto their camp, he sought one of his own.

Tamerlane wakened well before sunup to discover it was snowing, and he came shivering out of his bedroll. Close at hand, the bronc stamped an impatient foreleg at the barren ground under the pine trees. How was it, Ash wondered as he tugged on his boots, that a mountain man could survive a long winter up here. Out beyond the shielding canopy of thick green branches a biting wind swirled the thin layer of snow about and struck at Ash donning the sheepskin. He grimaced up at the greyish sky, and despite the early hour he could tell that it would be a clear day.

With his bedroll under one arm, and holding the saddle and saddle blanket in the other hand, Ash warily approached the bronc still stamping at the ground and by the glint in its eyes wanting to take its displeasure at the weather out on its rider. It nipped at Ash's arm when he reached out with the blanket.

"I don't cotton to cold either, hoss," he said edgily. Once the blanket was in place, he settled the saddle on the bronc's wide back and tightened the cinches. Securing the bedroll behind the saddle, he placed a cautious boot in the stirrup and swung aboard the bronc, to have it move out kind of stifflegged.

Still strong in him was the urge to build a fire and have some hot coffee, which he knew the nightstalkers

68

would be doing before too long. It had been a stroke of luck his checking on Irish Joe Finney's wagon train, since up to now the forays of the nightstalkers had been to take captive lone travelers or small parties coming in to Alder Gulch, and afterwards to scatter so they wouldn't reveal the location of their gold mine. Once he located the mine, Tamerlane knew that he needed the help of either the U.S. marshal over at Salt Lake City or the contingent of cavalry stationed northward at Fort Benton. Just as important to Tamerlane was finding out who ramrodded the nightstalkers, for this person would sooner or later return to Virginia City and check in with those he took orders from. Although Sheriff Plummer and his deputies were involved in this, he felt that perhaps that gambler, George Banefield, was a key figure in the criminal activities of the Cartel. But he needed more than just the barkeep over at the Anaconda Saloon telling of seeing the gambler and the sheriff out lurking in some alley on a rainy night.

As he rode, the blustery wind kept hammering away and yowling, with the bronc fighting the reins but otherwise striding out. Around him rose huge chunks of mountain shredding off wisps of cloud as it slowly lightened into day. But in the encirclement of those peaks stacked on all sides, and where Tamerlane rode, were meadows hemmed in by forest and rocky pinnacles. Already the ground snow was melting; higher up on the peaks it lay in ancient greyish shapes as of glacier ice. Cresting an elevation, he pulled up and gazed down into a mountain valley generally following the northward thrust of the Tobacco Roots. Along the way he'd been searching for the nightstalker's trail, would probably spot some hoof marks as the day

69

warmed up.

Aloud he voiced his thoughts while pulling out the makings, "We've been through a heap together, hoss. But still don't trust one another a whole lot. There's too much mountain for one man to cover in a day. And those who raided that wagon train are just hired guns—men who don't give a hoot in Hades about nothing. Just so's they get paid." He struck a wooden match into flame against his belt buckle and brought it with cupped hands to his mouth to light the cigarette. It was then Tamerlane's scanning eyes settled upon a tendril of smoke trickling skyward about where the valley sloped into mountain again.

Reining to his right, he went along the ledge looking for a crumbling spot that would give him access to the valley, to shortly come across one along with tracks left by the nightstalkers. Down on the valley floor, the bronc whickered thirstily as it veered toward a creek singing across a flower-spangled meadow. While the bronc drank its fill, Ash refilled his canteen. Looping the straps of the canteen over the saddle horn, he stood there and determined his course of travel along the valley. Long ago he'd lost any notions of recklessly rushing into something. Though he was above average when it came to handling guns, every nightstalker had probably been weaned on one, and having no scruples to speak of, would backshoot Tamerlane if the opportunity presented itself.

A covey of sharp-tailed grouse scurried into a thicket of bear grass at the approach of Tamerlane loping the bronc alongside a grey-twisted rock column. Further along blackbirds were rising above some birch trees, and now the bronc picked up the scent of something on the prowl and cocked its ears. Just as Tamerlane angled his horse toward the sheltering rocks, a couple of rifles cut loose. He left the saddle at a run and sprawled behind a boulder. The rifles kept barking, the slugs from them chipping away fragments of the rock sheltering Tamerlane. Crawling over to the bronc coming to a dead end amongst the rocks, he pulled out his rifle and climbed up to where he could fire back at the bushwhackers.

"Figured it was too easy my gettin' this close to them."

Around an occasional shot coming from the bushwhackers, he soon made out the dim outline of a horse shaded by pines, perhaps about two hundred yards further north. Cautiously he held his fire, squinting at the trees and rock-littered terrain in the valley. Tamerlane's vigil paid off when an abrupt movement came from the lower limbs of an aspen and he caught the sudden glint of metal. Without hesitating he levered four shells in that direction. A rifle fell into view as a man cried out in pain. Then the horse he'd spotted earlier vanished, and a moment later he heard the clatter of hoofs on stony ground.

Descending, Tamerlane climbed aboard his horse and used what cover there was to move upon the man he'd shot as he reloaded the Winchester. In among the trees he saw a horse drifting away at his approach and a man lying belly-down under a tree, and with the chilling wind poking curiously at Tamerlane as he swung to the ground, he levered a shell in the breech of his long gun. Stepping close, he stared without pity at the wounded outlaw, who stirred at Tamerlane's presence and managed to flop over onto his back.

"Mister . . . you busted me up . . . bad—"

"Just sending back some of your calling cards. Your partner vamoosed."

"Water—"

The nightstalker's sheepskin had two holes in it, one near his left side, another high in the chest, and both blood-stained. Showing above the coat collar was a black neckerchief similar to that of the demised Reno Lamont. "You're dying; water'll just kill you that much quicker. You were taking those muleskinners to your mine. Where is it?"

The nightstalker seemed to see some dark humor in Tamerlane's question, and his mouth quivered open and sardonic laughter spilled out. "You'll never find it! And . . . soon you'll be dead . . . same as me—" His head lolled to one side and he went limp.

When Ash Tamerlane rode out of the timber, it was into eye-piercing sunlight driving away the morning haze, and it had stopped snowing. Coming upon the tracks of the other ambusher, he cantered after them along the valley floor, and topping a rise, gazed at smoke rising from an old log cabin; there was also a crumbling shed and a large pole corral, empty and with its pole gate open. But the tracks he followed loped away from the cabin and to the northeast. He rode on in and pulled up by the corral. Though the snow laying on the ground inside the corral was disturbed, he figured only four or five horses had made those tracks, which meant the main party of nightstalkers had stopped only to take a breather last night, then kept on the move.

"This snowfall has sure enough hidden their trail," he mused bitterly.

Reining around, he went over to the cabin to find the

ground chewed up where three men had mounted their horses and ridden around the log cabin and southerly. "Two men tried to take me out—the other three are heading south, can't have left more'n a half-hour ago. Which means they heard those shots."

Something told Ash Tamerlane these men were heading back to Alder Gulch to report to the man calling the play for the Cartel. On the other hand, he could follow the other ambusher, but no telling where he'd go.

Reining the bronc ahead, Ash Tamerlane said grimly, "About the only way to kill a rattler is to cut off its head!" And with the wind pushing at his back a vengeful Tamerlane began pushing hard upon the track of the nightstalkers.

NINE

Yesterday Frank O'Neal had gone over to that livery stable looking for Ash Tamerlane to be told by the man owning it he'd hired another hostler, that he hadn't seen hide nor hair of a grey-bearded man such as O'Neal had described since earlier in the week. After that O'Neal had poked about town seeking this mysterious Tamerlane. Oftentimes his thoughts returned to that eerie encounter at the livery stable, the fact Tamerlane knew of his misdeeds back in New York. Here he was, Ash Tamerlane, a man of obvious breeding, looking to find those who'd done him wrong, saddled him with the moniker, Chain. If what Tamerlane had said was true—that a bunch of outlaws calling themselves the nightstalkers was actually kidnapping men and forcing them to work in some hidden gold mine—it would take more than Frank O'Neal or a Tamerlane to stop them.

At the moment O'Neal stood lounging under the arcade in front of the Virginia Hotel. The unexpected snowfall had served to remind him summers were short up here, and this would be no place to winter. Common sense dictated he get aboard the Walla Walla Express leaving at noon for Salt Lake City. He could always find employment there, or in San Francisco.

But he couldn't leave, and he knew it. He was trapped, partly by his own greed, the unsettling thought that either Tamerlane or someone else might just decide he hadn't revealed fully the dying statement of that highwayman. Then once again one Frank O'Neal would be visiting the preparation room over at T.O. Smithson's Funeral Parlor.

"Might I have a word with you, sir?"

Much to O'Neal's surprise the editor of the *Montana Post,* Thomas J. Dimsdale, had sought him out. O'Neal had learned that finances had forced Dimsdale to leave England for Canada, then to come here last year. Under the black frock coat Dimsdale had on a heavy cloth vest, round-collared shirt and bowtie. On his pallid face lingered a reserved smile. He had a receding hairline and his brow was always knitted into a frown. The bowler hat sat squarely on his roundish head, a sort of precise mannerism of aloof men.

"You might?" responded O'Neal in an equally soft tone of voice.

"We have made inquiries about you, Mr. O'Neal."

"Is that a fact now—" There was a brief flare of anger in the Irishman's eyes, an impulse simply to walk away.

"And we feel you can be trusted."

"We, sir, could mean just about anybody," he said cuttingly.

"I'm sorry, Mr. O'Neal, but at the moment I can't mention the names of my associates. We would appreciate your coming to a meeting tonight at—"

"Tonight I'm escorting a lovely lady to the opera."

"The opera doesn't start until eight o'clock. Please, Mr. O'Neal, it's important you tell no one about this. We'll be getting together over at Henry Gilbert's Brewery right after sundown. We . . . We intend to form a protective committee."

Chuckling, O'Neal said, "Don't you mean a vigilante committee?"

"Precisely, sir."

"And the we you're referring to are the other merchants—"

"Among others. If word gets out about this before we"—worriedly the newspaper editor glanced around —"before we get organized, certain criminal elements might resort to violence."

"Which is something I'm trying, at all costs, to avoid myself. This sounds intriguing, Dimsdale." A smile touching his lips, O'Neal tugged at his ear lobe, a thoughtful gesture. "Have you informed the illustrious Sheriff Plummer of your noble intentions?"

Thomas Dimsdale's eyes widened in alarm, and he said, "The sheriff is one of the reasons we have to do this. Will you come to the meeting?"

"Certainly, sir," said O'Neal. Here was a chance to tell Dimsdale and his cohorts of his past experience as a detective, and if handled right, he could make some money out of this.

"I say!" exclaimed Dimsdale. "Do I hear cattle?"

Now both men turned and gazed upstreet and beyond to cattle appearing on the upper reaches of the gulch along with a few outriders, and others saw the cattle too, and shouts went up. Up here, beef was a prime commodity, and O'Neal said, "Wish I owned those cattle."

"They'll bring a high price."

"Is that herd from Texas?"

"That's what I've heard. Well, Mr. O'Neal, until tonight." Quietly the editor of the *Montana Post* drifted away.

The saloons and business places and dance halls began emptying out, only to have these people scurrying back into buildings when the front riders began working the large herd toward the wide street. One of the cowpunchers, a big man wearing trailworn gear and astride a black horse having white markings at its fetlocks, loped in ahead of the approaching cattle. And Frank O'Neal, who'd been working his way along the street, paused in front of the Wells Fargo office when the waddy veered his horse over to intercept Sheriff Plummer just coming off a side street.

"You the local law?"

"I'm Sheriff Plummer. Glad you made it."

Shoving a sweat-stained hat to the back of his head, the waddy said bitterly, "You won't be too happy about what I've got to tell you, sheriff. Down in the Gallatin Valley we passed a wagon train that had been set afire. Some of the wagons were still smokin', so's I reckon this must have happened this morning or last night."

"That must be Irish Joe's freight wagons. Did you find any survivors?"

"All me and the boys come across was two graves. Maybe all these rumors are true about there being no law hereabouts, sheriff!"

"This is my town, mister," bristled Sheriff Plummer. "Talk like that can be mighty unhealthy."

"You threatening me—"

78

"Just a friendly warning. So you and your boys just don't get out of hand." Wheeling around, the sheriff strode downstreet and ducked into a saloon when the first of the cattle surged past.

Across the street, O'Neal had found the sanctuary of a dry goods store as the cattle flooded along the street tearing up boardwalks and hitching racks, and with the Texas waddies returning the waves of bar girls. There'd be a lot of celebrating tonight, the usual amount of violence.

But what disturbed Frank O'Neal at the moment was the almost callous attitude of Sheriff Plummer. At least forty men trailed out with Irish Joe Finney's wagons. Now that cowpuncher had told the sheriff only two graves had been found. Meaning that thirty-eight others just couldn't disappear. Plummer was duty-bound to go down into the Gallatin Valley and conduct an investigation. Unless, as O'Neal suspected, the sheriff already knew what had taken place. Come to think of it, hadn't he seen two of Plummer's deputies heading out yesterday or the day before? Yonder sheriff would bear closer watching, mused the Irishman, as his eyes chanced to land upon some boxes of hard candy displayed on a table. Picking one out, he turned and spoke to one of the clerks gawking out at the passing cattle, "Son, I'd like to buy this box of candy."

"That'll be two bucks."

"Back east I can buy a suit for that."

"Not out here you can't."

With a shake of his head O'Neal forked over two silver dollars telling the clerk to gift-wrap the candy and have it delivered to his room at the Commodore.

As the last remnants of the herd trotted past, he stepped outside. It had warmed into a pleasant summer day, though clouds covered most of the sky, and most of the snowfall had melted. It was almost two-thirty by his watch, and O'Neal went down to the Anaconda Saloon. There, he returned the scrutinizing nod of a gambler named George Banefield. As he recalled, Banefield had been over at the Commodore Hotel that rainy night. The fact the gambler had been in the company of the sheriff over at the Commodore added fuel to O'Neal's estimate of the man. Nodding at a few acquaintances, he lingered at the bar until one of the players at Banefield's table got up and left, then O'Neal stepped that way.

"I hear this is a no-limit game."

A merchant, judging from his rumpled brown suit, said, "Supposed to be. Sit in, Mr.—?"

"O'Neal."

"I do believe you're residing at the Commodore."

"For the time being, yes." His eyes took in the other players, two miners, a Union Army corporal, and Banefield.

George Banefield spoke up. "Seems we're going to have fresh meat for a change." Then he gazed studiously at the Irishman while dealing out a hand of stud poker. After this, Bandfield concentrated on the game, buying an occasional round of drinks, and playing somewhat recklessly as if money had little meaning to him.

Around five o'clock one of the barkeeps came back to light the coal oil lamps. Shortly after that into the Anaconda came three men to settle around another table. Right away O'Neal had them sized up as hardcases. He'd seen the bigger man, Boone Helm, over at the Commodore in the company of the beauteous Wyomia Blair. O'Neal's inquiries revealed that Helm was a parttime guide and payroll guard for the Webster Mining Company located further south near Summit City. About the woman he knew little, but the fact she was acquainted with Boone Helm didn't speak well for Wyomia Blair. Oftentimes outlaw gangs used women to elicit information from bankers or money men.

Glancing out a front window sometime later he realized long shadows were threading brazenly along the street. But it was George Banefield who cashed in his chips first and left the saloon. And when he did, O'Neal, glancing over at the table occupied by the hardcases, saw that Helm was gone too, the two other men still lingering over their drinks.

Out in front of the saloon, he looked about for any sign of either the gambler or the hardcase, somehow knowing the two men were involved in unlawful work. As the game had progressed during the afternoon, and although Banefield had made no overt threat, Frank O'Neal knew his life could be in danger. The gambler and possibly the sheriff were involved in a high risk venture, and the only man, O'Neal sensed, who could stop them was this Tamerlane.

Now he became aware of the tin rattle of piano music, of horses tied along hitching rails, of the sun being down and the sky hazing into night. Though he was hungry, O'Neal set a course for Van Buren Street and Henry Gilbert's Brewery. He would listen to what that newspaper editor and his friends had to say, and if profit was to be gained, so much the better. There was also the growing feeling in Frank O'Neal that the more friends he had the better. If these nightstalkers could take out an entire wagon train, what chance did a detective on the lam have against them.

Recalling the night he left his room at the Commodore in order to replenish his liquor supply, "You were right, my dearly departed father, my drinking habits could cause harm to more than my kidneys."

TEN

"Whatever possessed you to do it, Helm?"

"I'm ramrodding the nightstalkers!"

They were in George Banefield's room at the Commodore, having arrived at the hotel by different routes. Banefield had removed his suit coat and dropped it on an overstuffed chair, and he paced the floor now while loosening his tie, the anger he had for the hardcase stoning his eyes. Coming to work for the Cartel had changed Banefield from a gambler on the drift to a man eying his future. At his fingertips he had power, the money to enforce it, or by the mere snapping of a finger he could order a man killed or others taken with impunity, for up in the Tobacco Roots he was the law, both judge and jury.

"We needed supplies!" Banefield raged on. "Those men up at the mine can't eat gold bullion! You should have attacked Finney's wagon train after it left Red Lodge."

83

Baring his yellowed teeth in an angry grimace, Boone Helm crossed over and filled a glass from a bottle of imported brandy. He set the bottle down hard, glared over at the gambler. "Working with you is no picnic."

"Boone," he snapped back, "you're working for me. Never forget that!"

"Sure, sure." In his eyes flared a veiled contempt.

"I heard, Boone, that you and Finney were sparking the same woman," he said thoughtfully. "Also, that she cottoned to him more'n you. That must be it. You just couldn't wait to kill him, could you, Helm!"

"You're wrong, tinhorn. Finney's up at the mine with the others. But someone followed us out of the Gallatin Valley. Don't worry though, we gunned him down up near that old trapper's cabin."

"Who was it?"

"Never seen the body."

"It could have been . . . Chain?"

"Could have been. If so, he's out of our hair."

"I want to make sure. You knew him down in Colorado."

"Yup; just a spunky kid. Figured we killed him back there. Got lucky, I reckon."

"When you go back up there, I want you to dig up the body and make certain it's him."

"My men," he said flippantly, "don't make it a habit to bury who we kill, Mr. Banefield."

"No, I suppose not." Around a tightlipped smile he filled another glass with brandy.

"Wondering too, Banefield, just why you got me playing up to that woman, that Wyomia Blair? Too high-flutin' for my tastes."

"She might be willing to work for us."

"All she's looking for is some long, lost love. Wants me to check on this fella down at Bannock, other places."

"Yeah, Boone, man name of Ash Tamerlane."

"You know somethin' I don't?"

"Tamerlane's that spunky kid you thought you killed down in Colorado."

"The one we named Chain?"

"That be him." Placing his empty glass on an end table, Banefield added, "I doubt if Tamerlane knows the woman's here. But she's our bait, Helm. She'll reel him in sooner or later, that is, if Chain's still alive."

"Banefield," he sneered, "I don't see as how one man can go up against us. Maybe you're making too much of this."

"It isn't me who wants him dead, Boone. I have to take orders, same's you do. Right now, though, my major concern is getting some supplies up to the mine. Know for a fact there's another supply train coming in from Salt Lake. You know what to do."

After Boone Helm had taken his departure, the gambler began preparing himself for an evening that would include going to the Piper Opera House, where the famous Lola Montez was appearing. But his real reason for going was that Wyomia Blair would be there, having overheard her talking last night in the Commodore's spacious dining room. The truth of the matter was that George Banefield had fallen in love with Wyomia, an unsettling happening since in his travels he'd encountered many women. This in no way

85

had anything to do with the Cartel's wanting to get rid of the man she'd come out to find, the elusive Ash Tamerlane.

Every so often George Banefield would ride south out of Virginia City and report to the owner of the Webster Mining Company. Jason Webster, he'd soon found out, was oldish, in his late sixties and bound to a wheelchair, the most cold-blooded man the gambler had ever encountered. It had revealed itself in the quivering voice and the half-lidded eyes observing the gambler through the folds of seamed flesh covering the bony skull. Webster was a charter member, he'd learned by piecing together bits and shatterings of their few conversations, of a mysterious group of money men called the Cartel. Always the Cartel was seeking new mining ventures, ruthless men to do their bidding. The money offered Banefield to head up the Virginia City operation had been staggering, but so had the things he'd been asked to do, and without questioning these orders upon penalty of death. Not only had he signed papers to that effect, but the eeriest happening of all had been when Jason Webster made him place his right hand upon an open bible and swear a blood oath that he would never betray this trust. It was as if the prince of the air of the earth, the Devil, had been conducting this brief yet frightening ritual.

Reflecting back on it, the gambler realized it had been sacrilege—Jason Webster using a bible that way—and anyway, there was little he could do about it now. For the operation was running smoothly, with the gold mine up north starting to bring in real paydirt.

Here in Virginia City he had few problems to cope

with, though Sheriff Henry Plummer had only last night demanded more money for his services. And there was the Tamerlane affair. Other than that, Banefield thought smugly, he had little to concern him. So, closing his mind to the demands of the Cartel, and Boone Helm, he let images of Wyomia Blair filter in.

ELEVEN

"The candy was a nice touch, Mr. O'Neal."

Smiling into the eyes of Molly Carver walking arm-in-arm with him along Wallace Street, Frank O'Neal replied, "Simply sweets for a beautiful woman. So, Molly dear, have you come up with anything?"

"Just the usual gossip, Frank."

"That's better. I hate the formality of surnames."

"I've taken to wondering about a woman residing at the Commodore, a Mrs. Blair."

"Why's that?"

"Because of her involvement with a man named Boone Helm. She's trying to hire him."

"As a guide?"

"Yes, to help her find someone."

"I'm afraid if Helm ever got her outside the city limits that just might be the last we'd see of Wyomia Blair. I saw Helm earlier today, over where I was playing cards at the Anaconda Saloon. Banefield was there too,

Molly. He isn't all that good a gambler."

"But he tips lavishly," she smiled.

"I've the feeling Banefield is mixed up in crookedness . . . and perhaps with Boone Helm."

"I know something else about George Banefield," she said coyly as they turned the corner onto a side street and began crossing toward the opera house. "The man certainly has eyes for Mrs. Blair."

"Interesting? Although, Molly dear, I'd go for her myself . . . that is, if you hadn't chanced along."

"Mr. O'Neal, you've got a sugar-coated tongue."

Inside the opera house, O'Neal guided Molly Carver through those crowding the lobby, mostly miners, and some of the cowpunchers who'd shown up with that herd today. The building still reeked of new paint and a piney scent, since it had been rushed into construction earlier in the year. Passing into the theater, at Molly's suggestion they found seats near the back. With the arrival of eight o'clock everyone flooded to find seating, with O'Neal glimpsing George Banefield, and a few rows further up, Wyomia Blair talking to a woman employed at the Commodore Hotel.

The interior of the Piper Opera House was gaudy, containing side balconies and heavy red brocaded curtains and a high tinny ceiling in a rounded style. Below the raised stage a man sat before a high-backed piano. Now the house lights dimmed as the curtain started rising.

Whereupon out trotted a man to announce that, "Miss Lola Montez would be performing her famous *La Tarantula,* the Spider Dance!"

Whispered O'Neal, "Saw her perform this back

90

in New York. Lola pretends she's being attacked by some spiders; it's very suggestive, if you catch my meaning."

As the actress Lola Montez clad in a skimpy costume and other performers danced onto the stage, Molly Carver murmured, "I believe I do."

Engrossed in the performance, Frank O'Neal felt a stir of movement to his left as a late arrival sought a place to sit down, and finally crowding in next to O'Neal, the stranger whispered, "Enjoying the show?"

There was no mistaking that voice, and quickly O'Neal swung startled eyes to the passive face of Ash Tamerlane. "Until now I most certainly was."

"Let's palaver out in the lobby." Tamerlane rose, and trailed by Frank O'Neal, he went up the aisle and entered the empty lobby.

By lamplight he could tell that Ash Tamerlane had just come in off the trail; the growth of stubble on the man's face also revealed this fact to the Irishman. "Those Texas cowhands came across what was left of Finney's wagon train."

"I was there shortly after it happened. The night-stalkers took Finney and his men up into the Tobacco Roots. Lost their trail in a snowstorm. Had a shootout with some of them; then I followed three others back here. You come up with anything?"

"The trouble is, Tamerlane, that a lot of outlaws roam around Alder Gulch. No telling which ones are involved with the nightstalkers. Got bad vibrations about a gambler, Banefield—the man hangs around with some bad characters."

91

"Boone Helm, you mean. Helm's one of those I followed here. Saw him leave the Anaconda Saloon, also Banefield. Later they got together over at Banefield's rooms in the Commodore while you attended a meeting over at that brewery."

"Seems not too much gets by you, Tamerlane," he said grudgingly.

"Around here I'm known as Jim Benning, cattle buyer. How's about you keeping an eye on Banefield. I believe he's the key to the nightstalkers' operation, their paymaster. And he's connected to Sheriff Plummer. And speaking about the law, are those merchants going to form a vigilante committee?"

"They're damned determined about doing it. Want me to join up?"

"It sure won't hurt your social standing any. That woman you're with, isn't she a waitress at your hotel?"

"Molly's agreed to help."

"Won't hurt none. Meanwhile, I've got a chore to tend to."

"Boone Helm and his men?"

"Maybe."

"You'll keep in touch?"

"No maybe about that."

And just before turning to leave, Ash gazed over O'Neal's shoulder at one of the doorways opening onto the theater, for with the lilt of piano music came a strange, whispered intuition that someone from his past was in there. But during the last few years he'd steeled himself against moments such as this, growing

92

hard inside, not wanting to let that hard killing edge be swayed by foolish reminiscing. And flinty of face, Tamerlane left.

Those three hardcases hadn't made any attempt to keep an eye on their backtrail, so there were times on the way to Virginia City he could have picked them off. Once Boone Helm hooked up with that gambler, Tamerlane knew he'd made the right choice. While the last he'd seen of the other nightstalkers was them floating from saloon to saloon over on Van Buren Street.

It hadn't been Helm down in Colorado but another hardcase ramrodding the nightstalkers. Over in Jackson Hole country there'd been just Tamerlane and the outlaw Odie Davitt in a sixgun showdown, along with having it out with a couple more who'd done harm to his family.

Over on Van Buren Street, where some drunken waddies were staggering out of a dance hall as Tamerlane passed, he stepped to avoid them. Further along one of Sheriff Plummer's deputies loafing in front of a hardware store eyed Tamerlane with unmasked interest, then sauntered after the cowpunchers reeling across the street toward a saloon. In Ash's opinion towns like this lived hard and died quick. He'd bet a waddy's monthly wage on that deputy sheriff having paper out on him.

Where the street sort of levelled out, a few businesses were crammed together taking advantage of what space there was, among them a few saloons he sauntered in and out of. Then in a tent saloon set off by its lonesome he came across one of Boone Helm's men

93

leaning against the plank bar. Warily, Ash looked about for the man's companion or Helm himself before entering. As the night wind tugged at the canvas flaps and support poles, the sour stench of spilled beer rising with it to prick at Tamerlane's nostrils, he eased back of the hardcase.

Jabbing the barrel of his Deane-Adams into the man's back, he spat out, "Outside, hombre!"

"What the—"

Grabbing the man by the shoulder, he pulled him away from the bar and toward back flaps tied open. And when the grizzled-faced bartender made a grab for something hidden under the bar, Tamerlane barked, "Come up barehanded or loose an ear, mister!" He relaxed some when the bartender's hands shot up over his shoulders, his face turning almost the color of distilled gin.

"Pow!"

A slug just nicking Ash's hat brim brought him turning to face another nightstalker staggering gun in hand into the tent saloon, and to fire again. Tamerlane's weapon sounded and a spidery hole appeared in the hardcase's chest. The violent impact of the slug spun the man sideways where he became draped over a rickity table at which four miners were seated playing cards.

Meanwhile, upon spinning around and looking for the other nightstalker, Tamerlane caught only a glimpse of churning legs as the man bolted away. And out Tamerlane went. He fired, and the hardcase clutched at his thigh before tumbling against some empty packing crates. Somehow the hardcase managed

94

to unleather his handgun, a return shot punching a hole in the moon gliding overhead between some drifting clouds. Then he grunted when a slug from Tamerlane's weapon hit solidly.

"That's it, mister, no more!" he cried out, tossing his weapon away.

"Where's Boone Helm?"

"Seein' his woman."

"What woman?" Tamerlane edged closer.

"Sadie's her name; works over at the Frisco Bar." Still moaning in pain, he brought the hand clutching at his thigh wound down under cover to the uncertain light and pulled a hideout gun out of his dusty boot. "Damn you—"

"Pow—Pow!"

Ash Tamerlane's bucking gun punched out one eye and drove the nightstalker's Adams apple back into his throat. Moving in to stare without pity at the dead man, he murmured viciously, "Your kind never learn."

Turning now, he became aware of a crowd gathering, their excited shouts bringing others out of nearby buildings. Quickly he broke into the deep shadows cast by a warehouse. With the building between him and the tent saloon, he hurried over to an alleyway and went south to Cover Street. That hardcase had forfeited his life when he went for that hideout gun. He wanted more than Boone Helm's present whereabouts. From that nightstalker he'd wanted the location of the Cartel's gold mine. And before the stroke of midnight, Tamerlane mused grimly, Boone Helm would tell him what he wanted to know.

95

Detouring into a general merchandise store, he was informed by one of the clerks that the Frisco Bar was at the other end of town and on a side street. Outside again, he reloaded the Deane-Adams. To his surprise there was a slight tremoring of hand, and this gave Tamerlane pause, made him realize that even killing scum didn't come natural.

"It's got to be this way," Ash told himself. "I've got no other choice."

Etching a determined look on his face and holstering his revolver, he set out up the rising street. Tonight the town seemed crazed with a lusting need to celebrate the arrival of that trail herd. Gold dust would be thrust into the greedy hands of barkeeps and merchants in exchange for overpriced goods, and it didn't matter too much to a lot of miners anyway, figuring tomorrow or the next day they'd hit that big strike. Up past Alder Gulch, in another valley and high where a creek came twisting out of a canyon, Tamerlane had located his secret camp. Once in a while he'd do some panning in the creek just to give himself living money. His needs being simple, it left him ample time for the task at hand.

He came to the end of Cover Street and the last side street upon which raucous noise and lamplight poured out of the Frisco Bar; it wasn't much of a building, just the falsefront and the two floors under a flat roof. As he crossed over, a freight wagon drawn by oxen trundled past, and while pausing Tamerlane had a sudden premonition of danger. Another of Boone Helm's friends could have witnessed the shooting of a few minutes ago and hurried up here to warn the outlaw.

But he also considered that Helm had never set eyes on him before. Tugging at his hat, Ash moved toward the batwings just as a miner staggered out through them and reeled against the hitching rail. Cautiously Ash stepped up and peered inside the saloon. Though a few poker tables were occupied, most of the gambling action seemed to be centered around the roulette wheel, and there was no sign of the outlaw. He shouldered inside. At the bar, he glanced around, still gripped with uncertainty.

The lone barkeep sidled over while wiping his hands on a grimy apron that was really an empty flour sack tied around his belly. He gummed at an empty tooth socket as Tamerlane motioned toward a bottle of Carstair's Best. Then Tamerlane swung his attention to a bar girl swivelhipping down the staircase. She slipped around those crowding the roulette wheel and up to the bar, her long, black hair framing olive skin and black eyes sort of caressing Ash Tamerlane, and in Spanish she said, *"Buenas tardes, Senor."* And placing the tray she carried on the nicked bar top, to the barkeep, "A *botella* of whiskey for Senor Helm."

"Same to you, *senora,*" said Ash. "Been kind of looking for *Senor* Helm."

"You don't look like a *bandito.*"

"I'm working on it. What room's Helm in?"

"Upstairs where his woman is crying."

"Obliged," Ash said around an appreciative smile. With the eyes of the Mex woman still holding to him, Tamerlane began threading around the tables. The staircase ran up to about the height of a six foot man before splitting so's those a'wanting to satisfy their carnal needs with one of the bar girls could go up either side. On the back wall between the staircase hung the head of a moose punctuated with a couple of bullet holes, the glass eyes glittering at Tamerlane passing upward. Touching onto the hardwood floor in a narrow corridor, he stared through pale light wafting from a coal oil lamp at the open window, and with the evening breeze stirring a grimy curtain. As he hesitated while deliberating over which one of the five rooms lining the corridor had the hardcase as its occupant, a woman screamed, to be cut off by the sound of a hand hitting flesh. Tamerlane hesitated, burred with unease, but finally he went on until he came to a door through which seeped a woman's deep sobs.

The knob turned silently in his hand as he palmed his sixgun. Shouldering into the unlighted room, it took Ash a couple of seconds to locate the woman sprawled in almost naked disarray on the bed, but by then it was too late. A pickaxe handle slamming into Tamerlane's left shoulder threw him forward. From the opposite side a second ambusher brought the pickaxe handle he wielded down to knock the gun out of Tamerlane's hand. He choked down the cry of pain as a blow to his back drove him into the wall. But he managed to spin around and evade a handle arcing at his head.

"Get out of here!" one of the men shouted at the woman, and she scrambled out of the room.

The same man grunted in surprise when Tamerlane sprang forward and drove him back into the dresser. Somehow he brought the ambusher spinning around and clawed out the man's handgun just as another weapon tore a hole in the oozing blackness; the man shielding Tamerlane stiffened in shock. Tamerlane's gun started bucking, the two slugs staggering the other ambusher.

"We'd best get in there!" someone shouted out in the corridor.

"Stinson, what the hell's going on in there!"

Shoving the wounded man away from him, Tamerlane bent to retrieve his Deane-Adams and cast away the ambusher's sixgun. And without hesitating, a long stride carried him toward the closed window, then he dove through it shattering glass and wood. Yelling as he fell to drive the air out of his lungs, he hit the ground hard near the east wall of the saloon. He lay there stunned, still retaining his grip on the revolver, though his hat was gone. That brief stop at that dry goods store had delayed him just enough to give Boone Helm's accomplices time to get here first and set up this ambush. And by now Helm was long gone.

"He went out the window!"

"Stinson's hit bad!"

Someone came to stand framed in the second-floor window as Tamerlane struggled up from the ground, and with the man upstairs yelling, "He's getting away!" Then he began firing after Tamerlane breaking into a run.

Still groggy from those blows and the fall, Ash Tamerlane came reeling down an alley and over to a rain barrel squatting alongside a shed. Bracing himself on its wooden staves, he plunged his head into the icy water to clear his thoughts, the shock of the

99

water tingling his skin. He flexed the muscles in his left shoulder while probing for any broken bones.

"Wait a minute? Stinson? Yeah, he's one of Plummer's deputies." He punched an angry fist into the water, the bitterness making him forget the pain, a sense of frustration surging through him. A dog slinking past snarled at this intruder and loped away.

"Maybe I should just lope away too," Ash muttered. "Helm and his men have stacked the deck."

Complicating matters was the fact he'd shot and probably killed a lawman. Come sunup Sheriff Plummer would have his men out scouring the town for cattle-buyer Jim Benning, which meant discarding that alias. He moved on in the direction of his boarding house. There, he removed his upper garments and used a towel to dry himself. Along with the livid welt at his shoulder his gun hand still felt numb. But Tamerlane knew he'd just lucked out.

He lay down upon the bed and watched moonbeams dance in through a window, trying to chase away some lonely thoughts as he puzzled over his next move in this deadly game. His first priority was to find Boone Helm. He doubted the man would leave Virginia City tonight. Sheriff Plummer or others involved with the nightstalkers could be hiding the hardcase, who by now would have figured out it was Tamerlane who'd gunned down the other hardcases and deputy Stinson.

That narrowed Ash's search down to one man—gambler Banefield. In his opinion George Banefield was no more'n a hired lackey, just another opportunist, one of those eastern money men who'd come out here to be bossman of the Cartel's crooked operations.

Pushing up from the bed, Ash lighted a lamp and sat down before the dresser. He began applying the makeup which would place him once again in the disguise of the hostler. It was getting late, edging past eleven, and when Banefield returned to his rooms at the Commodore Hotel, the one called Chain would be a'waiting him.

TWELVE

To Wyomia Blair the performance over at the Piper Opera House had been a scandalous but enjoyable evening out on the town. And for this evening at least she'd pushed aside her reason for coming out here. In the past few years her written inquiries to other mining towns as to the whereabouts of the man she loved had proved fruitless. This search for Ash Tamerlane had been costly. She knew he was alive, though others claimed he'd perished along with his family down in Colorado.

Here in Virginia City, Wyomia couldn't shake this odd premonition that her search would end. Hindering her attempts to find Ash Tamerlane was the cold hard fact that everyone out here seemed to be more interested in mining gold than hiring on as her guide. All except for Boone Helm, a rather foreboding appearing man who'd made a vague promise of helping her.

After that argument with Ash, so many, many years ago it seemed to her now, it had been all too easy to throw herself into the arms of another man. Suddenly she found herself a married woman, and discovering too late she didn't love her husband. The marriage had lasted two stormy years. Wyomia Blair's search for the only man she could ever love had taken much longer.

Still puzzling Wyomia was a conversation she'd had with one of her father's business acquaintances back in New York. Quite callously, as a matter of fact, the man had told of his investing in a Colorado mining venture. Jason Webster had gone on to say that all Wyomia had to do was venture out there herself and pay her respects at the gravesite of Ash Tamerlane buried next to his father. And so she had. Only to discover that Ash's grave was empty. She learned no more than that in the Paradox Valley where Coloradans seemed reluctant to tell of what had taken place. Upon returning to New York, a determined visit to the offices of Jason Webster only brought the information he was gone, wouldn't be back for several months.

But that empty grave could only mean to Wyomia Blair there was conspiracy here, and that her love, Ash Tamerlane, was still alive. That sustained hope had carried Wyomia Blair westward to Alder Gulch as the news of the gold strike made banner headlines back east.

It was from a woman who worked here at the Commodore, and who'd accompanied Wyomia to the opera house, that she'd learned that another man residing at the hotel was a private investigator.

"And so, Mr. O'Neal," went on Wyomia Blair, "now you know my reason for coming out here."

"Interesting to say the least," smiled Frank O'Neal. "Yes, indeed, Mrs. Blair, an empty grave would arouse certain suspicions. Ash Tamerlane, an interesting name." He was seated around a table in the barroom of the Commodore with Wyomia Blair and Molly Carver. While the women were sipping from coffee cups brought in from the dining room, the Irishman was drinking brandy. Other than this only two other tables were occupied and a handful of men stood along the bar.

"Mrs. Blair," said Molly Carver, "you mentioned having this Boone Helm help you—"

"He seemed rather rough, and somewhat untrustworthy. But who else could I turn to." Wyomia's widely-spaced eyes dusted with mascara rested again upon the Irishman. "Except for you, Mr. O'Neal?"

This was the last thing Frank O'Neal had expected, Wyomia Blair wanting to find Ash Tamerlane. Musing about the other side of the coin told him that Tamerlane had in all probability forgotten about the woman, though O'Neal's eyes taking in Wyomia's singular beauty told him this was highly unlikely. Perhaps Tamerlane had learned of Wyomia's marriage, had left it there. At the sound of footsteps he turned his head and suddenly George Banefield was there, sweeping off his hat and murmuring politely, "Well, Mr. O'Neal, a pleasure seeing you again. May I join your table?"

"Ah, by all means," said O'Neal as he rose. "Mrs. Blair, Molly, this is George Banefield—another guest of the Commodore."

The men settled down at the table, with Banefield telling of having attended that performance at the opera house, and asking the barkeep, when he stepped over, to bring another round of drinks. "I do hope you ladies will forgive my being a gambler."

"How interesting," said Wyomia around a guarded look at the newcomer.

"This is a very . . . unsettled place," Banefield said. "It disturbs me how a wagon train, Finney's, could be attacked like that. I'll certainly miss him. How do you ladies manage to cope with news like this?"

"I can't speak for Molly," said Wyomia Blair, "but I feel our local sheriff hasn't done all he should to stop this kind of thing."

"I'm afraid, Mrs. Blair, the sheriff and his deputies aren't enough of a force to wipe out the many outlaw gangs operating in the gulch. Truly we need sterner measures."

Molly Carver, after she'd cast a guarded glance O'Neal's way, said, "Just what could be done, Mr. Banefield?"

Waiting until the barkeep had set down their drinks, and he'd paid the man, Banefield said, "We could ask that a cavalry unit be sent up here. Sorrowfully, the Civil War still rages on. Seems the U.S. marshal is involved elsewhere. What, Mr. O'Neal, would you suggest?"

Here it was, pondered Frank O'Neal; it was now plainly evident he'd been observed while talking to the editor of the *Montana Post,* and that Banefield probably knew a meeting had taken place in an attempt to form a vigilante committee. The results of that meeting had been tentative at best; some were firm in their decisions to go ahead with it, the majority of a wavering bent of mind. A honed instinct voiced its opinion that seated across from him was the man behind the sinister activities of the nightstalkers.

"What would I suggest?" O'Neal smiled with his eyes. "Back east we'd have more coppers walk the beat."

Into George Banefield's eyes came a sudden glint of anger—was that a warning for the Irishman?—and then Banefield was directing the gist of his talk toward Wyomia Blair.

Seated there, O'Neal gave Molly's hand a reassuring pat under the table, as unraveling to him was the gambler's real intentions of intruding upon their table. The gambler had strong and unmasked feelings for Wyomia Blair. That she had formed an instant dislike for George Banefield was evident to everyone else there but this intruder.

Idly, his resentment over Banefield's unexpected presence growing, O'Neal became aware of another man entering the barroom and striding quietly over to a far table. Glancing that way, O'Neal's contenance lost that look of idle disinterest when he realized it was Ash Tamerlane in the guise of the hostler.

Their eyes held, briefly, as Tamerlane's slid first to Molly Carver to flint upon landing on the gambler. And only then did recognition stab at Ash to flare open his eyes. O'Neal could see the pain and anguish playing across Ash Tamerlane's face as he stared across the barroom at Wyomia Blair, the disbelief at her unexpected presence slowly diminishing, and then with an abrupt suddenness he rose lithely and hurried out a side door.

"Frank, what's wrong?"

"Nothing . . . Molly."

"Strange," piped up Wyomia Blair, "but that old man who just left reminded me of . . . someone."

107

"Just another drifter, Wyomia; nobody to be concerned about."

Later, Frank O'Neal was to wonder why at that precise moment he had lied to Wyomia, or perhaps it was the presence of the gambler which had held his words. Later, too, he found himself swept into sudden violence, but by then it was too late to tell her Ash Tamerlane was alive, for Wyomia Blair had vanished.

THIRTEEN

Once again Frank O'Neal found himself at T.O. Smithson's Funeral Parlor staring with other members of the vigilante committee at the body of a young man stretched out on a table in the back room. It was around four in the morning, Thomas Dimsdale, the editor of the morning paper, having stole into O'Neal's room at the Commodore to inform him the committee was finally going into action.

Just as troubling to O'Neal was the disappearance of Ash Tamerlane. Somehow he had expected Tamerlane to keep in closer touch, but by now Frank O'Neal had learned better than to try and discern the man's next move. One thought stayed with the Irishman: if Wyomia Blair hadn't been in the barroom of the Commodore, Tamerlane would have accosted the gambler George Banefield.

Gathered around the table were grim-eyed men, sobered with the realization that once they started this thing they were in it to the end. The talk on the way over here had been mostly of Sheriff Plummer's brazenness as he openly defied those who'd put him into office. Some of these men felt the sheriff had been involved in the murder of Nicholas Thalt.

A slug had entered young Thalt's forehead just above his left eye. On the dead man's wrists and neck were the marks of a small lariat, and now Dimsdale spoke up.

"The man who found the body said that Thalt had been dragged through brush while still alive and then been dispatched, for he was still clinging to sage brush."

"Do you have a suspect?" inquired O'Neal.

"We know who murdered him."

Thomas Dimsdale said, "Piecing together the testimony of the man who found Thalt's body, we're reasonably certain a man named Long John is the murderer. Presently this man and others are camped in a wickiup someplace near Wisconsin Creek. Well, gentlemen, let's take our departure."

Trooping outside, the vigilantes climbed aboard their horses. The horse under Frank O'Neal was skittish, a green-broke bronc, unsure of both the saddle and its rider. At a command from Dimsdale the small cavalcade of fifteen riders headed raggedly down Van Buren Street which was battened down for the night. Leaving the town behind, they cantered along the stagecoach road following the downward slope of Alder Gulch.

It was fairly evident to O'Neal, after they'd bypassed a couple of smaller mining communities and were now on that part of the gulch opening onto the Ruby Valley, he wouldn't be keeping this morning's meeting with Wyomia Blair. At which time he was going to tell

110

Wyomia that Ash Tamerlane was alive, and in fact, close at hand.

The merchants and miners came splashing across Wisconsin Creek in the uncertain light and through blackish ground shadows, and breathing deeply of the cold mountainous air, then exhaling it thick as buttermilk toward mist floating amongst underbrush. Out in front was the miner guiding the vigilantes, armed as most of the others were with rifles or scatterguns, and handguns tucked into belts and stiff holsters. The rest of the story, young Thalt's selling a span of mules to his employers, Burtchery & Clark, had been narrated to O'Neal as they rode by Dimsdale. After getting paid for the mules, Thalt had gone to Dempsey's Ranch to bring up the animals, only to be set upon by his murderer.

"I see their wickiup just up ahead!"

Breaking toward some willow trees, the vigilantes slid to the ground and tied up their horses. They spread out and came in on foot to find four men sleeping in bedrolls outside a makeshift building covered with brushwood. Dimsdale, clicking the hammer back on his scattergun, fired one of its barrels at the brightening sky, and another merchant shouted to the stirring outlaws, "We'll take you out if you try for your weapons!"

"Which one of you is Long John?"

An outlaw with black hair matted to his head snarled, "That's me. Who in tarnation are you men?"

"We accuse you of murdering Nicholas Thalt!"

"It wasn't me what done that dirty deed," the outlaw cried out as the vigilantes pulled him away from his comrades.

111

"We have a witness that will testify otherwise."

"Then he lies!" shouted Long John, squinting away from the edge of the sun appearing over the Tobacco Roots. "George Ives done it—I'll swear to that."

"Is Ives still here?"

"Sleeping in the wickiup."

A couple of shots rang out tearing brush away from the top of the wickiup. Shortly, three men stumbled out to stand uncertainly in the growing light, and Long John pointed out Thalt's murderer.

Upon finding out that the men capturing him were merchants, George Ives spat out, "You gents been deputized by Sheriff Plummer? If not, this is an illegal act . . . a breech of my privacy."

"You'll sing a different tune when you're dancing on air, Ives!"

"No!" Thomas Dimsdale shouted. "I want Plummer, and others who defy the law, to know that we mean business. Since there's some question here as to who murdered Thalt, we'll take them all back to Virginia City."

"What proof do you have?" questioned George Ives. "There are a lot of outlaw gangs hereabouts. And some of these men chanced by to spend the night." A sneer showed yellowed teeth poking through an unkempt mustache.

As if in response to the outlaw's question, a mule braying brought everyone's eyes to a nearby knoll, and the miner who'd guided the vigilantes yelled, "That's Black Bess alright. Nick Thalt sure thought a heap of that mule."

"Ives, that's all the proof we need. A couple of you round up the mule and the others can't be far away."

112

Frank O'Neal set about tying leather thongs around the wrists of an outlaw before heaving the man aboard his cayuse. The excitement of what had happened was thinning out, and he felt tired but strangely drawn to the vigilantes. He realized he'd gained the respect of the merchants, which should stand him in good stead if he decided to go back into business as a detective.

Hemming in the outlaws mounted on their horses, and with the mules along, they loped southward toward Wisconsin Creek. As he rode, it suddenly struck O'Neal this part of the mountains would see him again, and though puzzling over this, he began sorting out various landmarks.

The passing of the vigilantes caused miners to glance up from where they were working their claims in the muddied waters of the Stinking Water flowing through Alder Gulch. Past Nevada City they rode, dust from their wearied horses rising from the stagecoach road, finally coming around a bend and straightening some in their saddles as they touched onto Cover Street. Some of these outlaws were known to the townspeople of Virginia City. Now, their unarmed presence amidst armed merchants and miners served to stir up a town daydreaming the morning away. Out came more and more locals to stare silently at a new breed of law.

The appearance of Sheriff Plummer out of his jail office brought the vigilantes to a halt, with their spokesman, Thomas Dimsdale, folding his hands over the saddle horn as the sheriff stepped toward him.

"Dimsdale, you know you're operating outside the law!"

"Something you seem to be familiar with, Plummer!"

"You should have informed me you were getting

113

some men together to form a vigilante committee."

"Wisely, I didn't." He reined his horse around. "All of these men are outlaws. But we won't be the judge of that. They'll receive a fair trial."

"For doing what?"

"For starters, Plummer, that man, George Ives, murdered young Thalt. Long John'll swear to that in a court of law. We'll be putting our prisoners in your jail. So, sheriff, a word of warning—make sure none of them escape!"

Frank O'Neal, after going with the other vigilantes over to a livery stable and tending to his horse, tiredly made his way to the Commodore. What he'd become involved with had given him new insights as to the courage and determination of the merchants to rid the gulch of outlaws, a new look at himself. Perhaps he could be accepted in Virginia City despite his past activities, but staying here meant keeping involved with the vigilantes. There was also O'Neal's involvement with Molly Carver. He'd found her to be a strong-willed woman, somewhat attractive, a homey type as his mother had been. And looking forward to seeing Molly, Frank O'Neal entered the lobby, detoured into the dining room and found an empty table. Suddenly, he was ravenously hungry for some food, and a glimpse of Molly Carver.

When she did appear, it was to hurry over to O'Neal's table and settle down to his left, the drawn look on her face telling him that she'd been worried about him, and that perhaps something else was amiss.

"Something's happened to Mrs. Blair!" She reached

114

out for his hand. "She's gone, Frank! One of the maids went up to clean her rooms. There were signs of a struggle. And some of her clothes were missing."

"When did it happen?"

"Late last night."

A regretful sigh passed through his lips. "Now she'll never learn that Ash Tamerlane came into the barroom when we were there. He was disguised as a hostler."

"She does know, Frank. I thought it would make her feel better knowing he was alive."

"You don't suppose he abducted Wyomia? Hardly. Without my morning coffee thoughts come hard, Molly dear."

As she rose and hurried back toward the kitchen, Frank O'Neal knew with a frightening certainty that the nightstalkers had come for Wyomia Blair. Could this have been by order of George Banefield? The man was dangerous, would let nothing stand in his way, not even Wyomia Blair's cool disdain of his fawning intentions. He could also recollect Tamerlane telling of his father investing a large sum of money with some eastern investors before heading out to Colorado. That must be it. These investors, or the Cartel as Ash Tamerlane had called them, probably were aware of Wyomia's search for the man she loved. As did gambler Banefield. Since they had tried and failed to murder Ash Tamerlane, by abducting a woman he'd once considering marrying, the nightstalkers could flush Tamerlane out into the open. Tamerlane had mentioned a gold mine—this must be where they'd taken Wyomia.

Almost immediately Molly Carver returned bearing a tray holding a pot of coffee and a plate of steak and eggs. She set the plate in front of O'Neal and said, "I don't suppose it'll do any good to tell the sheriff?"

"Hardly. Tamerlane's been gone almost three days now. And I haven't seen the gambler around town either. Molly dear, something's up."

"What can we do?"

"I haven't the foggiest."

"There's the vigilantes, Frank. Perhaps they could go out looking for Wyomia?"

"I seriously doubt it, Molly. We'll have to be the ones who do something about it. Which means I've got to find Tamerlane."

FOURTEEN

The men he followed out of Virginia City had surprised Tamerlane by striking to the south along Alder Gulch. They were five in number, hardcases led by George Banefield. It was Tamerlane's original intention to pick off Banefield's men, then have it out with the gambler. But the hard way the men he trailed were pushing their horses had told Tamerlane that something out of the ordinary had stirred Banefield away from the saloons and gambling dens. Pondering over this, he concluded the gambler must have been summoned by the real bossman out here.

He'd been stunned to see Wyomia at the Commodore, and in the company of George Banefield. Where had she come from? After Tamerlane had bolted out of the barroom, he'd returned to the boarding house, packed his gear, and left. Though Frank O'Neal had also been seated there, the question burning at Ash Tamerlane was whether or not Wyomia could actually be working for the Cartel. This would explain her presence out here. Time, he'd noticed, had worked few changes in a woman he'd once loved, and for the moment and in order to survive, any notions about Wyomia must be pushed aside.

As his habit was, Tamerlane's alert eyes took in the deep bluish sky riding high over the Tobacco Roots. Deep as he was in the gulch, he could only see limited patches of the Gallatin Valley to the east, chiefly just piney trees sweeping past him and the rocky terrain of the mountain. Once in a while during his silent passage, there had drifted over the sounds of miners working claims in the Stinking Water and lesser tributaries.

Easing onto a granite outcropping, he left his horse ground-hitched away from rimrock, and with field glasses in hand, he hunkered over for a closer look at what lay ahead. First he scoped the distant and shimmering outline of Summit City tucked in a gorge. Closer, the gambler and his men were picking their way across a small creek, and then making tracks for French Gulch. Viewed by Tamerlane through the glasses were massive wood-frame buildings making up a working mine. That heavy rumbling filtering up to him could only be a sixty-stamp mill breaking down gold-bearing quartz. On the western lip of the gulch he could make out the snaking mouths of two mines, with a mule pulling an ore car coming out of the north one. Only money men could finance an operation of this size, which to Tamerlane meant the Cartel.

As the gambler and the hardcases swept into the buildings, movement along a ridgeline to the northwest caught Tamerlane's eye. Moving from a hunkering crouch into a more comfortable sitting position, he glassed a string of pack mules passing through a notch just below a snow-capped peak. He could feel the excitement building, certain that the mule train had set out from a hidden gold mine a day or two ago. An operation of this size would need more gold ore than those two mines below in French Gulch could provide. Proving this would be another thing, since those working here drew a daily or weekly wage and headed home at night. No sense, he mused bitterly, dragging a U.S. marshal up here.

By the sun he figured it was around midafternoon. Reaching for the makings, he noticed a puzzling plume of smoke rising skyward along the southern reaches and high up on the gulch wall. Through the field glasses he stared in surprise upon a mansion perched on a rocky foundation, the tops of the trees in the gulch brushing near its foundation, along with a long series of stairs with handrails leading up to its eastern wall.

"The lair of the bossman!" Tamerlane said grimly.

By nightfall Tamerlane knew intimately the layout of the mine, those guarding it secure in their belief they could overcome an attack by some roving outlaw gang. There were around thirty men guarding the mine buildings; up near the mansion less than half a dozen were keeping watch. Tired of coldcamping as it cooled into night, Tamerlane was eager to get on the move.

He reined the bronc away from the outcropping and found a slanting downslope bringing him onto a grassy meadow. Dismounting by the creek which the gambler had crossed earlier, he let the bronc slake its thirst. While refilling his canteen Tamerlane keyed his ears to the sounds and light coming from the mining buildings, maybe a quarter of a mile further west. Pinpoints of light came from the mansion. Which to Tamerlane meant the gambler was up there reporting to the man bossing the Cartel's western investment. He had it in mind to find a way up along the southern reaches of the gulch so's to enable him to leave the bronc close at hand. And one way or another, tonight he meant to square accounts with some of those who'd killed his family.

One of the servants, a tall, imposing mulatto, glided into the anteroom occupied by George Banefield. His name was Domingo, a Jamaican, and Jason Webster's major-domo. The mulatto's passive, ebony face didn't reveal the contempt he held toward Webster's hired hands, which was what he considered the gambler, someone the man he worked for would use and discard. The room they were in held its secrets, as did other parts of the house, behind thick curtains hanging mutely over the windows. The western-style furniture was sparse, just a few handbacked chairs and a settee and the varnished log walls.

"This way please." The mulatto's long strides carried him ahead of the gambler through several empty rooms and finally to a double door, whereupon he opened one and stood aside so that Banefield could pass inside. Closing the door, Domingo went over and entered a small room, where he removed a picture from the wall and placed his eye against a peephole.

The gambler, moving toward a large mahogany desk, said, "I assumed I came here to see Mr. Webster—"

"Jason Webster went back east on business," replied

Hoyt Parker, a solid oak of a man, balding, with a raspy way of speaking and clothed in a worn black suit. He was in charge of the mining operation in French Gulch. Before that there'd been mining jobs in South America, Nevada, and Colorado. Without preamble he added, "Why haven't you gotten rid of Tamerlane?"

Banefield felt a stir of resentment as he eased onto a chair. "It isn't because we haven't tried."

"Then we'll get rid of Tamerlane the same way moths are attracted to light. Meaning that old flame of his, Wyomia Blair."

"Kill her?"

"Later, maybe. Have your nightstalkers take her to the hidden gold mine. Then get word to Tamerlane. He'll damnwell go looking for her."

"That should flush him into the open," responded the gambler as he folded one leg over another and shaped a conspiring smile for Parker. The truth of the matter was he'd fallen deeply in love with Wyomia Blair. She was a woman of uncommon beauty, and breeding, and she'd made Banefield realize that life was more'n gambling dens and hard liquor. She had only confirmed his decision to cut and run from Alder Gulch. Part of the wages paid to him by the Cartel he'd deposited in a Virginia City bank; there were other bank accounts in Salt Lake City and San Francisco. Once he withdrew his money from that Virginia City bank, however, it was with a dreadful certainty he realized word would be carried up here; but he wasn't about to leave almost forty thousand dollars behind. Now the gambler pushed thoughts of Wyomia and leaving aside as Hoyt Parker began detailing the urgency of acquiring more pack animals.

"North at Caribou Gulch they're close to hitting the mother lode," said Parker. "That ore'll have to be brought down here for processing. Unfortunately we just don't have enough pack mules, horses. Nor enough men up there to get at that ore."

"That'll mean having the nightstalkers operate more. Boone Helm and his men will want more money. Theirs is a risky business."

"So's ours, Banefield! I've received word that district sheriff Jim Williams is starting to poke his nose into what's going on in Virginia City, and what we're doing here. It won't be too long a'fore he figures out we've been processing too much gold ore . . . and maybe, just maybe, Banefield, he's gotten wind of our pack trains coming in from the north."

"I could have him killed."

"For now, Jason Webster has been against it. And dammitall, Webster's a hard man to work for." Rising, Parker went to a side table and filled a couple of glasses from a decanter of brandy. Fetching these back to the desk, he handed a glass to Banefield before settling down again. "Here's all this gold . . . and us a'gettin' just a monthly wage. I want more'n that; figure you do too, Banefield."

"Say it plain, Parker."

"There's been talk of them organizing a vigilante committee over in Virginia City. This happens, won't be too much longer before we'll be out of business. This operation I got in mind is tailor-made for two men smart as us. The gold we process here is shipped by wagon train to Cheyenne—then by stagecoach to Denver. I've got privy to the time of shipment and routes. Would be an easy matter for your nightstalkers

122

to waylay some of these shipments. Bring the gold to a spot I've got picked out."

A cunning smile dancing upon his lips, the gambler said, "You're a larcenous sort same's me, Parker. What kind of a cut do you have in mind for me?"

The answer to George Banefield's question came in the form of a gun being cocked as Ash Tamerlane eased into the room. The bluster on Hoyt Parker's face slowly faded away, an inbred caution telling him he would die if he went for the gun holstered at his right hip.

"Banefield," said Tamerlane, "I hear you've been looking for me."

Half-rising, and twisting to look toward the door at Tamerlane, he said shakily, "You're him, ain't you, the one called Chain—" Now a muted command from the Deane-Adams brought Banefield's hands up and moving away from the desk.

"That's better," said Ash. "If I heard right, you're making plans to steal some gold bullion—just a couple of turkey vultures stealing from another." Cold fury was etched into Tamerlane's set features, but it wasn't these men he'd come to kill, but would if they resisted, and he spat out, "I want Jason Webster!"

"Tamerlane," said Hoyt Parker, "you'll never get away from here. You must know this is an armed camp. And I have to admire your tenacity in getting this far. One shot from your gun and my men'll be swarming in here. Be reasonable, give it up, man."

The barrel of his Deane-Adams centered on Parker's midriff, Tamerlane said viciously, "I want Webster, now!"

Just in time Tamerlane detected the evasive glint in

Parker's eyes. Spinning sideways, the slug meant for him grazed Tamerlane's ribcage before slamming into the man standing behind the desk. As Hoyt Parker, a surprised look showing on his face, crumbled toward the desk, the Deane-Adams was cutting loose at the mulatto desperately trying to fire back at Tamerlane. Though he knew he'd scored a hit, the mulatto was stumbling away. And when Tamerlane swung around to locate the gambler, the man had fled out another door. Stepping up to the desk, he lifted the dying Parker up by a shoulder hold.

"Where's Jason Webster?"

Chortling laughter, blood seeped out of Parker's mouth. "Gone . . . back east. But the . . . woman's here—"

"Woman?"

"Your . . . old flame, Tamerlane. Remember . . . Wyomia? Taken by . . . by the nightstalkers to . . . other mine." Then death claimed Hoyt Parker.

With wondering thoughts of Wyomia filling his mind, Tamerlane went to a window giving him a clear view of the gulch floor. Several armed men were running toward the long staircase winding up to the house. Tamerlane had left his bronc in a hidden cul-de-sac higher up on the gulch wall, had been forced to move in stealthily to bypass at least four men watching the house.

Moving out of Jason Webster's cluttered office and its eerie, mediciny smell, and warily into a hallway, his eyes stabbed past a marble statue for any sign of the mulatto, or George Banefield. On the hardwood floor were several crimson blotches, some trailing down the hallway. When a door was wrenched open in the western reaches of the house, Tamerlane hurried into a bedroom just as a bullet found the door behind him; he realized the mullato was still alive. Prying open a window, he slipped through it and into the inky night.

The gulch wall Tamerlane climbed along was sheer, rocky, sparsely covered with trees and underbrush, offering him little shelter. Desperately seeking rimrock, he heard a man below shout, "Up there!" And searing pain lanced into Tamerlane's left side followed by the heavy report of a Winchester. Without hesitating, though staggered some, he managed to spring over the rough rock edge. A laboring run brought Tamerlane to his bronc. Struggling into the saddle, he spurred the bronc due west so as to angle northward around French Gulch. For certain they'd be after him, and since these men were familiar with the country hereabouts, Ash reckoned his chances of getting away were slim at best. But it was better than no chance at all, or lying back there dead.

As he clung to the saddle, Tamerlane's probing fingers revealed the lead pellet was still lodged near the back portion of his side. And though the numbing effect of it striking was wearing away, he had no choice but to ignore the growing pain and dizziness, letting the bronc find a cantering route along the rugged sweep of mountainous terrain.

"Anyways," came his voice so tinged with bitterness it drove some of the darkness away, "Wyomia's got to be working for the Cartel."

For how else would it explain her and that detective, Frank O'Neal, having a round of drinks with the gambler over at the Commodore Hotel when he'd slipped in there. He should have never trusted the

125

Irishman. As for Wyomia, the notion she could be involved with a man like Banefield didn't ring genuine to Tamerlane.

So it pretty much came down to O'Neal hooking up with the gambler, and with Ash musing that money was the divining rod by which these men judged their loyalties. Where had George Banefield gone? Certainly he wouldn't hang around French Gulch. That meant he would head back to Virginia City, hook up with the nightstalkers, and maybe make tracks for that hidden gold mine. Which was where Ash Tamerlane knew destiny was heading him.

Conjuring up amongst a cloudbank hanging low over a distant peak was an image of Wyomia, moonlight setting it to glowing, and at that moment Ash realized he cared more for her than he wanted to admit.

FIFTEEN

Drumming along with Frank O'Neal, coming on horseback onto a Douglas fir seared and shattered by lightning, was the concern of Molly Carver that he remain in Virginia City instead of traipsing mountainward in quest of Ash Tamerlane. Back then, two days ago, he'd cast aside Molly's fears, crammed his saddlebags with possibles and set out into the unknown. Along the way he'd managed to avoid a band of marauding Indians, Bannacks, from a description given to him back at Virginia City. His passage through the mountain valleys, crevices, streams and stands of timber, cradled beneath the barren peaks above timberland, had forcefully brought home to the Irishman that he was out of his natural habitat. Saddlesoreness and an overwhelming stiffness also told O'Neal that.

"North," Tamerlane had told him, "northward through the Tobacco Roots somewhere is a place of death, a living hell for those captured by the nightstalkers."

There had been marks left by shod hoofs he'd come across, stamped into loamy soil or in the form of deep-sucking holes left along muddy creek banks. Of white men he'd seen no sign.

With his mind set on nooning under an inviting stand of birch trees, O'Neal was coming across a meadow when he spotted a pole corral, and quickly reined up the grain-fed horse he'd rented from a Virginia City livery stable. The front door of a weathered log cabin stood open, and he decided to go on. Around the cabin he came upon freshly-churned ground and droppings, and to the north, hoofmarks littering a slope passing down into a small mountainous valley.

At his approach, a coyote bolted away from a creek that cut through hard, rocky ground. Dismounting by it, he saw under its clear surface the outlines of brown trout. Tiredly he reached up and took off his hat, grimaced at the sweat staining its greyish felt crown. Thonged behind his saddle was a new sheepskin coat; another purchase had been a Henry rifle. But if trouble came, O'Neal knew he'd be no match for men used to this deadly way of life.

"Do I owe Tamerlane this much?" he asked dejectedly. He gazed through weary eyes at the endless reach of mountains. Nighting up here hadn't been much to his liking, this huddling around a campfire that sooner or later would be spotted by the night-stalkers. Back in New York there'd been times when he had to find someone in other towns, but close at hand had been hotels and a willing damsel or two. Uncorking his canteen, the faint smell of brandy wafted into his nostrils before he slaked his thirst. Then

128

it suddenly occurred to the Irishman that his searching eyes had caught a glint of smoke or reflecting metal. From his high vantage point he stared due north, wondering if at last it could be Tamerlane, or perhaps that hidden gold mine. On this arduous journey, too, had come to the Irishman an appreciation for the rugged beauty and danger up here, that a man rode his horse with caution and slowly. When the sun poked out lazily from behind a spongy white cloud, he suddenly realized it would be dark in another hour or two, and he headed out again, seeking to pick up hoofprints and a haven for the night.

Irish Joe Finney, dragging cold mountain air into his gasping mouth, ignored the jabbing thistles as he snuggled deeper into the thorny clump of snakeweed. He could hear those searching for him coming up the ravine, cursing and shouting to one another. Secured to his ankles were steel rings bound together by a length of chain. His eyes burned defiantly out of a face thinned to the bone with a matted beard, and hair coming down to his heaving shoulders. Some of those who'd been captured with him were dead through lack of food or simply being worked until they dropped. The soles of his boots had worn away, and his flight up from the canyon where the mine was located had brought him over sharp rocks and pebbled ground, but he had more to worry about at the moment than gashed feet.

Irish Joe had been brutalized with whip and chain, and endured. He'd known some of the men guarding him, some disgruntled miners taking on with the nightstalkers or hardcases drifting in for a piece of the action. Someday, Finney had vowed, there'd be a day of retribution.

By Finney's confused reckonings he was north someplace in the Tobacco Roots. This afternoon, as he toiled away in the depths of the mine, he'd overheard one of the guards saying a woman had been brought in. And tucked away in Finney's embittered memory file were the names of Boone Helm, the gambler Banefield, and others.

The branches of an aspen stirring just downslope brought Finney's head away from the small opening he'd created at the bushes, the light from the torch the guard held revealing the cocked rifle as it wavered here and there.

"See anything?"

"Just a damned owl."

"Do we bring this one back alive?"

Boone Helm shouted back, "Finney's going down! I doubt if he got this far yet. Alright, alright, spread out more and we'll work our way down the gulch."

As torchlight and the scuffing of boots on the gravelly track sought lower elevations, Irish Joe Finney emerged from the brush and began laboring along the steep pitch of the gulch. Once it levelled off, he saw before him under moonlight still more trackless waste, that land forming a high plateau under peaks touching the stars. But he plunged on, knowing that at first light they'd be after him on horseback. Soon the night and Finney were as one, the harsh cold taking huge chunks of his reserve, the plaintive wail of a lobo wolf spurring him on in strides shortened by the binding chain. On the slope of a broken swell he glanced upward and froze, and only when his head cleared did Finney realize it was the twisted remains of a juniper, blackened, a skylined alien creature as were other junipers he stumbled past in the near-darkness. Loneliness pressed down upon the weary Finney, the haunting fear he would die up here, and hunger gnawed at his belly. But Irish Joe stumbled onward, southward, he thought.

Sometime later, three hours or more, he brought his weakening frame over a fallen Douglas fir and past others unruffled by any wind. Then, the light which he gazed upon was in the shape of a campfire glowing alongside a pond surrounded by reed, and with limber pines just beyond. Hunkered near the fire was a man who'd just wrapped his teeth around a hunk of dried beef, and quickly Finney swung back amongst the trees. He prowled around until he found a broken tree branch, then he tore away a few smaller fingers and stole through the trees.

A whicker from his horse gaped open Frank O'Neal's eyes. Reaching over, he grasped the Henry, and in fear-instilled tones uttered, "The nightstalkers must have found me." Spinning onto his side, he crawled away from the fire to drape himself behind an aspen. Glancing at the horse, he saw that it had swung around and was staring uptrail.

Without warning, and at a lumbering run, the club held high, Irish Joe Finney broke out of timber and came screaming the short distance to the campfire.

O'Neal shouted, "Far enough!" Somehow he remembered to level a shell into the Henry's breech.

Spinning that way, Finney stared wildly into the muzzle of the rifle, and he cried out, "Kill me and get it over with!"

For the first time O'Neal noticed the leg irons, and too, there was something familiar about this wild mountain man. "I'll be . . . damned. You're that muleskinner . . . Finney?"

"You damned well know who I am . . . you murdering scum."

"I'm not one of them," insisted O'Neal. And suddenly he found himself tossing the rifle over to Finney. "There, man, I came out here seeking the one called Chain. He was taken same as you were, Finney. But down in Colorado."

Murder gleamed out of Finney's crazed eyes as he curled his finger around the trigger and settled the muzzle upon Frank O'Neal. "Chain? Aye, I've been chained." Now he seemed confused by what O'Neal had just done, and the barrel wavered.

"The man I'm talking about, the one called Chain, is Ash Tamerlane. He's out here someplace looking for that hidden gold mine."

"Is that . . . coffee I smell?"

"You need something stronger than coffee." Carefully he worked his way around Finney and to the campfire. Picking up his canteen, he pulled out the cork and held out his arm. "Brandy, my friend."

SIXTEEN

A fast-running stream known as Daylight Creek cut through Virginia City, polluted by the townspeople and miners, and swollen from last night's torrential rainfall. Just to the north of the creek on Wallace Street a body of men strode past a wagon sunken to its hubs in the mire. Most of them carried rifles, and two men had hanging ropes. Deliberately they'd gathered long before dawning at Henry Gilbert's Brewery, and among the leaders of the vigilantes had been Thomas Dimsdale, who realized once they set out on this dangerous endeavor there was no turning back. A lot of others he'd approached hadn't wanted any part of a vigilante committee in a region ruled by outlaws, and Dimsdale knew they feared for their lives. Turning onto shadow-strewn Cover Street, the seventeen men took notice of a miner ducking out of a building called the Chinese theater.

"Anyone recognize him?"

"Miller—got a claim just past Nevada City."

"Should we stop him?"

"No reason to," said Dimsdale. "He probably overpaid that Chinese whore anyway." A few vigilantes laughed at this, and fell silent again when Dimsdale nodded toward a large wood-frame building set back from the street. "That's Haze Lyons' boarding house."

"It's George Ives we want."

"But we'll hang Lyons too if he's in there."

"There'll be a trial," insisted Thomas Dimsdale.

"It'll just delay their hangings, but that's what we agreed on."

As the vigilantes split into two groups, one cutting down an alley to come in the rear entrance of the boarding house, the editor Dimsdale found himself once again thinking about the missing Frank O'Neal. He'd confided in the Irishman, and had finally come to the conclusion that O'Neal was involved with the highwaymen. This would explain O'Neal's presence at the dinner table with George Banefield over at the Commodore. Now Banefield had also left town, as had a woman residing at the Commodore, Wyomia Blair.

As a newspaperman, Dimsdale had weighed heavily the fact Frank O'Neal could merely be a victim of circumstances. The report he'd gotten from New York City Police Department told of O'Neal's criminal activities, along with a notation that a warrant had been sent to Sheriff Henry Plummer requesting he arrest the Irishman. Which, in Dimsdale's opinion, would never happen, since Plummer was too involved with running his own gang of outlaws. Out here a lot of men were dodging shady pasts, miners and outlaws alike. And in the days to come a lot of men would be dangling from trees, Frank O'Neal among them, a fact which saddened the editor.

The vigilantes shouldered through the front door of Ma Larkin's boarding house, a woman who'd ventured out from St. Louis. They fanned out along the first-floor hallways and crept up the staircase, while other vigilantes kept a watch outside. Randall, a sallow-faced merchant, went over and rapped the barrel of his scattergun against the paint-chipped door panes of the room occupied by the landlady, and after a few moments a bolt scratched back, with the angry sleep-filled eyes of Henrietta Larkin coming to recognize the merchant Randall before it came to her he was armed.

"Why, Mr. Randall, just what need do you have of a gun?"

"We're all vigilantes, Mrs. Larkin."

"My . . . Heavens!" Paling, she managed to fuss with her greying hair before peering past the merchant at the silent men lurking in her boarding house.

"We want Haze Lyons."

"There . . . that's his room."

"Do any of his friends stay here?"

Regaining her composure, she said testily, "How should I know? These kind of men come and go all the time . . . I . . . I do declare—" She slammed the door in the merchant's face.

A few minutes later it was determined by the vigilantes that Haze Lyons was another of those who'd left town. Gathering in back of the boarding house, Thomas Dimsdale spoke.

"We have Bill Palmer's statement that he found

young Thalt's body out near Ramshorn Creek. Which is about where Robbers Roost is located."

"Reckon you mean Daly's Ranch."

"One and the same, men. I've also learned that both Haze Lyons and Ives hang out there." He could make out the earnest determination etched on each face, the eyes expressing secret fears that maybe some of them wouldn't measure up. There was a certain camaraderie felt by the editor, of men not cut from the cloth of a gunfighter but willing to die to rid the gulch of these outlaws. They were men who'd simply grown bone-weary of living on the dangerous edge, unsure that maybe a new day would bring them down, or one of their family. They were men grown damned weary of having a crooked lawman lying through his teeth all the time. Right about now, figured editor Dimsdale, his fellow townsmen would buck a band of renegade Blackfeet and be damned to the consequences. Some-how, this notion surfaced, that all of them had matured into westerners, not cattlemen, nor waddies, or muleskinners or stagecoach drivers, but of the same breed. This notion also served to make the editor more confident of the weapon he carried, a Colt Navy .36 won off a drunken cavalry sergeant over at the Anaconda Saloon.

Coughing to clear his throat, Dimsdale went on, "Jim Williams, sheriff of the district, is on his way with some deputies. Coming in through the Ruby Valley. Since he'll be arriving later today, I suggest we get our horses and wait for him where the stagecoach road cuts out of Alder Gulch. It'll save us time getting to Robbers Roose."

A barkeep, Riley by name, said, "We started this vigilante thing. And none of us are chickening out. These outlaws have been calling the tune too long; and that includes Plummer and his bunch. I say we ride."

"Get your horses. We'll assemble over at the brewery."

"Yup, we'd best get out of town before the locals wonder what we're up to. And I'm speaking of Clubfoot George. He's been passing word to the outlaws whenever someone pulls up stakes and leaves the gulch. In my opinion the man's just as responsible when these folks get held up and killed as those a'doing it." Now the vigilantes hurried away to gather their horses.

For reasons of convenience, Thomas Dimsdale kept some horses stabled behind his newspaper office, and he headed that way. Coming onto a side street where the Commodore Hotel seeped light out of its dining room and kitchen, Dimsdale had the urge to go in for a warming cup of coffee. Then a side door opened and Molly Carver, pulling a shawl over her rounded shoulders, called out to him.

"Molly, is it?"

"Yes, Molly Carver. We get up pretty early around here, Mr. Dimsdale. When I saw you and those other men I knew this vigilante thing was more than talk. Frank told me about it, that you'd asked him to join."

"I assume you're speaking of Frank O'Neal." He brushed a finger along his mustache. "To be truthful, Molly, I've been entertaining dark thoughts about him."

"Because he'd been talking to George Banefield?"

"Among other things. I find it strange that he should suddenly disappear like this. Or maybe not. Did you know there's paper out on him?"

"I know that, Mr. Dimsdale. I also know he's a good man . . . though impulsive at times."

"Typically Irish. I'm pressed for time, Molly."

"Just a couple of minutes more," she said pleadingly. Then Molly Carver's narration of how she became involved with the Irishman began with a brief capsule of the night the dying highwayman had come into the Commodore. There was mention of Ash Tamerlane, along with the reason so many men were disappearing.

"A hidden gold mine?"

"Frank said it was someplace north in the Tobacco Roots. The same thing happened down in Colorado. Please, Mr. Dimsdale, you must believe me."

"Truly, Molly, I find this difficult at best to comprehend. These men call themselves the night-stalkers? And . . . and this man, this Tamerlane. He simply comes out of nowhere and makes these . . . wild statements—"

"But it's all true. I'll swear to it on a bible."

"Up north"—he swung a hand in that general direction—"encompasses a lot of territory. Territory which happens to fall under the jurisdiction of the U.S. cavalry. I fear, Molly, Virginia City has more trouble than she can handle." He turned to move on, paused and gazed back at her fighting back the tears. "I gather that you're in love with Mr. O'Neal?"

"That I am."

"He's a lucky man."

"A good man, Mr. Dimsdale, believe me."

"Perchance if we encounter one another out there I'll

138

hear O'Neal out. There's also the possibility he could be dead."

"I know he's alive!"

"Tamerlane you said? . . . A strange name?" And uttering that, Thomas Dimsdale passed from view around the arcaded front of the Commodore.

SEVENTEEN

Yesterday Ash Tamerlane had used his hunting knife to dig out the leaden slug from his side wound, afterwards to apply a herbal poultice and bandage the wound with a hunk of cloth torn from a spare shirt. Though there was some giddiness, he felt stronger, more able to cope with the jarring impact of his bronc traveling over boulder-strewn ground on a climb that had carried him far beyond Alder Gulch and that trapper's cabin where those nightstalkers had tried to ambush him.

A seasonal change was beginning to stir up in the mountains, the wind colder and knifing at him, while sweeping up to him out of a mountain valley came the bugling of bull elks fighting to gain exclusive control of a harem of females. Today a lot of cloud cover filtered out the sun, grey-tainted clouds which often heralded an approaching snowstorm. Slicing away at his approach went a red-tailed hawk, to hop aboard a wind thermal and soar upward.

Earlier in the afternoon he'd been sighting through

his field glasses this valley watered by creeks, when there appeared a man leading a horse upon which another man was stretched and tied down over the saddle. Also, on his northward hunt for the hidden gold mine, he'd come across three or four different trails which could have been used by the nightstalkers. Those he'd spotted had worked their way down into dense timber sprinkled along the valley floor. And Tamerlane was there now, his rifle cradled in one arm.

He'd run out of tobacco, and was down to his last hunk of beef jerky. With his body craving solid food, he knew that sooner or later he'd have to risk killing a deer, which were plentiful.

Clearing the aspens which lurked along a dry wash where, sparkling in loamy soil, were small leafs of gold probably carried down from watery runoff, he tugged back hard on the reins when he saw those he'd spotted earlier coming over a lump rise. Tamerlane exclaimed, "I'll be . . . it's that Irishman?" And loping ahead, he returned O'Neal's tentative wave.

"You're a hard man to find."

"Others have told me that." Sheathing his rifle, he nodded at the man on the horse. "Leg irons? Reckon he escaped from that hidden gold mine."

"It's Irish Joe Finney."

"The owner of that wagon train."

"And really bad off, Tamerlane. I came across him yesterday. Actually he stumbled upon my campfire. They sent some horsemen after Finney; around nightfall they gave it up. How are you fixed for grub?"

"Same's you, I guess. This is as good a place to night as any—yonder in them birch trees."

"Tamerlane, there's something you should know."

"Later, O'Neal. We need some venison."

Under a lee formed by cradling rocks beamed Tamerlane's campfire. On a spit made from trimmed branches hunks of venison were frying, the savory aroma wafting past Tamerlane and Frank O'Neal drinking coffee by the fire to Irish Joe Finney wrapped up in a bedroll.

"So you came out looking for me?"

"I get the feeling you still don't trust me?"

"Mr. O'Neal," he said bluntly, "I can't afford to trust anyone."

"Now you sound like me. It was because of the woman, Wyomia Blair, that I risked my neck looking for you. She's been abducted."

His eyes locked on O'Neal's, Tamerlane knew the man was telling the truth. And suddenly the taste had gone out of the coffee, a cold anger steeling his weathered contenance.

"That's the woman they brought up to the mine," Finney told them as he came weakly out of the bedroll and squatted down to Tamerlane's left. "Boone Helm brought her there. Overheard some of the guards saying their bossman, George Banefield, was there too."

"They're hoping to smoke me out." He tossed the empty cup down. "Got no other choice than to make tracks for Caribou Gulch."

"Back at Virginia City things are coming to a boiling pont. The editor of the *Montana Post* told me he was sending for the district sheriff. But even if Sheriff Williams doesn't show up, the vigilantes are taking matters into their own hands."

"Tamerlane, it'll be suicide you going it alone against the nightstalkers."

"Maybeso, Irish Joe, but that's the way it has to be."

"Dammit, man, it's my fight too! The fight of my men still held captive up there! Me and O'Neal get back to Virginia City, we'll bring back the vigilantes."

"Afraid I can't wait that long. Seems the venison's ready." Reaching to the back of his belt for his sheathed hunting knife, Ash sliced away a large portion of the hot fat-dripping meat and handed it to Finney, passed another hunk to the Irishman, O'Neal. "And afraid I judged you wrong."

O'Neal said, "It was Molly Carver who stirred up my sense of decency. No need to tell you that up here I'm out of my baliwick. And maybe back in Virginia City too."

"Your conscience stirring enough to make you head back home and give yourself up?"

Frank O'Neal laughed. "This mountain air hasn't made me that giddy of mind yet. San Francisco has a nice ring to it. A change of name and perhaps of profession would set me up just fine."

"Does that change of venue include Molly Carver?"

"It could." Around a mouthful of venison he added, "There's also Wyomia. Ah, I see by your expression you entertain certain doubts about the lady."

"Doubts still linger about you, O'Neal."

"The fact you saw me and Wyomia with that gambler. As a detective, it's sometimes wiser, and more profitable, to bring your enemy closer than your

144

friend. I believe Wyomia Blair came out looking for you, Ash Tamerlane."

"Perhaps," he said vaguely. His eyes slid to Irish Joe Finney. "I need to know something about that mine layout—"

"We were kept in a log stockade . . . and no roof to keep off that damnable rain. The guards stay in log cabins. Caribou Gulch snouts into a mountainside; the gulch being around three miles long, and narrow, maybe a couple of hundred yards. Just one way out of it to the east."

"I want to know the approximate location of the dynamite shack."

"Last building to the south—back half set into solid rock."

"Dynamite's touchy stuff," ventured O'Neal.

"Handled it down in Colorado," Tamerlane said. "Saw what happened to those who got careless. What's the general mood of those guarding the place, they the kind to get boozing some . . . or maybe over-confident?"

"That about describes Boone Helm's men A bragging lot, mainly about how fancy they can shoot. To my way of thinkin' they're like a mule fartin' in the wind. Liked to use those chains to cut flesh. So's I aim to get back up there and do some fancy cuttin' of my own."

"Tamerlane, I wish you'd reconsider going at this alone."

"Just too mulish to wait. Been searching ten years for those who murdered my family. Getting late, gents; you'll be needing all the sleep you can get."

Before sleep claimed Tamerlane he pondered over whether he should guide the others back to Virginia

City, as Finney's presence would tip the scales in favor of the vigilantes tagging along to Caribou Gulch. But Wyomia's presence there, either willingly or as a prisoner, had already made up Ash Tamerlane's mind. And as one used to the trail, moments later he fell asleep.

EIGHTEEN

The agonizing screams went on and on, and still Abe Wydell, a cattle rustler out of the Panhandle, kept lashing at the luckless muleskinner with a length of cruelly-biting chain. Under the watchful guns of other nightstalkers the others held captive could only stare angrily at the bleeding body of the muleskinner, and some of his bones had been broken too, so that he couldn't raise his arms to defend his shattered face from the coming blows, and with Wydell grunting and blowing out frosty mountain air everytime he struck.

Off to one side stood Boone Helm with his legs spread apart in a poise of arrogant defiance. Pleasure at what was taking place rippled in his eyes, and when the muleskinner went into convulsions and expired, Helm inhaled a satisfied puff of cigar smoke.

"We killed Finney up amongst those rocks," he lied. "And to show we mean business when someone tries to escape, that muleskinner had to pay for Finney's misdeed. We ain't all that heartless, though. There'll be extra food from now on, and blankets. Alright, herd 'em back into their stockade."

Long after the screams had died away the fear of what had just happened still caused Wyomia Blair's body to tremble. She fought back the tears of frustration, of what these savage men had in mind for her as she stopped pacing the rough-hewn floor and peered through a crack in a window covered with boards. There was no stove in the log cabin, and the thin blankets failed to keep out the penetrating chill of night. But this was something Wyomia could cope with. Her greatest fear was of being molested or killed, for it hadn't been explained to her why she'd been kidnapped. It had all seemed so brazen and unreal, those men stealing into her rooms and taking her that night. Her wrists still bore the marks of the ropes; the inside of her mouth had been cut when she'd been gagged.

That the man she loved was not only alive but had been seen in Virginia City seemed a miracle. Surely Ash would remember her? Had he found out about her failed marriage? Or after all these years would he still find her attractive? All because of some stupid argument they'd gone their separate ways. All because of youthful pride. Why, at the moment, she couldn't remember what they argued about. How handsome he'd been, so alive with a masculine vibrance, sharing with her that wonderful trip to Africa, and those European escapades. He would have changed, of course, after what had happened to his family.

"I cannot change the past," mused Wyomia Blair. "But I can truly do something about my future, and Ash's."

The moments of self-reflection reeled away to be

148

replaced by uncertainty when there came the sound of metal rasping against metal, and then the door was pulled open, and the man she'd once tried to hire as a guide stood there.

Through a smirk Boone Helm muttered, "Chow time, wench."

"That man you beat up—"

"Buried him with some others. You'll chow down with Banefield and me. And later, maybe, I'll have some pleasure with you." As she hesitated, he sprang over the threshold, and grabbing her arm, forced Wyomia out of the cabin.

"You . . . animal," she cried out.

Helm's response was to curse and backhand Wyomia alongside her hairline, the grip he retained on her arm keeping her from falling. "I like a wench has some spunk. Now, get along." Lustfully his eyes played over her full-bosomed figure.

He brought Wyomia Blair along the uneven gulch floor hidden as it was under the brow of Diamond Peak. Above them the mountain was a vast dominating force, tinged with patches of snow above timberline and darker than its western edges still lighted by the lowering sun. There was the stockade, just a circular structure made by sinking logs into the hard loamy soil and abutting, like the dynamite shack, against the granite wall of the gulch. Besides the cabin in which Wyomia had been held, there were five others strung to the east in the gulch and the pole corrals occupied by mules and horses. Westward, and poking into the mountain, was the gold mine. Wyomia's eyes took in the men standing guard, mostly near the stockade holding captive the luckless. One of the cabins had been turned into a saloon, from which came voices pitched in anger and drink.

"My men gotta have some fun," said Helm. "Wanna join them, wench?" He snickered as they cleared the wall of a cabin to come upon another setting under aspens, and with George Banefield emerging from it.

"Well, Mrs. Blair, we encounter one another under trying conditions."

Wrenching away from Boone Helm's grip, she said bitterly, "You . . . bastard! First this animal hits me— now I suppose you'll do the same?"

"I told you to go easy with her, Helm!"

"Easy ain't a word I comprehend, hombre."

"I suppose not," Banefield said scorningly.

"This means you and the wench are gonna dine alone?"

"Seems there is a glimmer of intelligence."

"Meaning?" Tugging at his gloved right hand, Boone Helm brought it to dangle menacingly over his holstered sixgun.

Bolstered by the presence of Wyomia, along with his desires for her, the gambler retorted recklessly, "You get my drift, Boone. There's more involved here than a man like you understands. A helluva lot more! We're merely pawns in this game, Boone. Those behind this mining venture don't want any of us to upset the apple cart. Meaning they can come down hard on us if you or me messes things up. We stand to make a lot out of this."

"Ain't you afraid," jerred Helm, "of telling me all of this in front of her?"

"I just want to clear the air, Boone."

"Roosting out here is pure hell. My men think

likewise. If these uppity-ups got all this money, just maybe we're being underpaid?"

"Something's come up, Boone, that'll make us both rich. It has to do with what happened at French Gulch. Meaning that Parker went down—and maybe that whole operation."

Slapping a wondering hand against the butt of his gun, the outlaw said, "This better be good—"

"Boone, if we hit the mother lode, we won't have to cart any ore down south. It'll be mostly pure gold ore! Power, Boone! That gold'll give us the power to do what we damned want . . . and to hell with Jason Webster and his rich cronies. We've got enough mules to cart that gold anyplace we want. Then we'll be the power brokers."

"To you money means power," came back Boone Helm. "All I've got a craving to do is head Argentina way and get me some Spanish women. *Como hacer gusta ellos manzanas, Senor* Banefield?"

"I savvy what you're saying, Boone."

"Reckon I'll just mosey over to the saloon and do oomo fancy card playing." Smirking at Wyomia, he added, "The gambler gets done with you, be a'lookin' for me."

As the leader of the nightstalkers swaggered away, George Banefield motioned for Wyomia to go ahead of him into the cabin. He ignored the contempt flashing in her eyes, but wanted her all the more, and knew he would possess the high-spirited woman. Wealth would give him Wyomia Blair, which was in the form of the gold ore being carried out of the mine on the backs of his captives. What had taken place southward in French Gulch told the gambler a new deck of cards had

151

been put into play. As of now he'd severed any ties with Jason Webster and the rest of those eastern money men. Discarded, too, would be Boone Helm once his usefulness was over; he relished the notion of putting a bullet between Helm's sarcastic eyes. As for Ash Tamerlane, he would have little chance against the nightstalkers. And to make certain the man was killed, come dawning Banefield would put a thousand dollar bounty on the man's head.

"I hope you like grouse, Mrs. Blair. Please, sit down. That wine was imported from France. And I do hope you'll forgive the table setting?"

"And if I decide not to humor you?"

"I hope you understand you're not in a very humorous situation. So let's act like civilized people . . . and then I'll explain why you were brought here."

"I suspect it's because of Ash Tamerlane—"

"It is. But the situation has changed, somewhat." Pouring wine into their glasses, he smiled at Wyomia, and there was a shading of greed in Banefield's voice when he told her about the mother lode they expected to find at any time. "There should be several million dollars worth of pure gold ore. We'll take it by pack train to Salt Lake City. Your friend, Tamerlane, is looking for those who killed his family down in Colorado. I had nothing to do with that. Once we clear this place for good, Wyomia, that gold will give me a lot of respectability. Believe me, a lot of the so-called social elite back east got their starts in like fashion."

"I'd prefer you calling me Mrs. Blair."

"I want you to share that gold with me."

"Heavens, Mr. Banefield, are you proposing?" She sipped at the wine.

"That will happen in time."

"You are an arrogant sonofabitch."

A hard smile splitting his lips, the gambler said, "And you're the most desirable woman I've ever met. Consider this, Mrs. Blair, that one word from me means you and Boone Helm get better acquainted."

"Seems your true colors are showing. I suppose you plan to kill Ash Tamerlane too?"

"If he tried to interfere with our mining operation, I have no other option. The grouse is getting cold. Shall we dine, Wyomia?"

NINETEEN

Last night the horse had gone lame, and it wasn't until they'd headed out again that Frank O'Neal realized it had thrown a shoe. This had forced Irish Joe Finney out of the saddle and hobbling along on foot. As Finney's condition worsened, they stopped to rest more often, and around noon circling specks in the sky brought this retort from Irish Joe.

"Damned turkey vultures. Frank, you've got to shoot this chain away. This stumbling around up here is no good."

"We'll give away our position."

"We haven't spotted anyone yet, back there. So get that rifle." Spreading his legs apart to draw taut the chain, Finney grinned at O'Neal's unmasked concern. "No way you can miss or hit me in the legs."

Butting the stock against his shoulder, O'Neal curled a nervous finger around the trigger and unleashed a round at a link of chain. Part of the link broke away;

155

another slug severed the link with the chain flopping down. While the horse began shying away and whickering its fear.

Finney grabbed the halter and said, "Easy now." He patted the horse on its neck and shoulder. "Well, Frank, it's a day and a half since we left Tamerlane. Since we're on the western slopes of these mountains, our best bet is to work down into the Ruby Valley."

"At least we'll be going downhill."

"There'll be water . . . and berries or acorns. Could risk going for an elk."

"How you faring?"

"Got gumption enough to take on these mountains. And them devilish nightstalkers. Walking'll be easier now. So, Mr. O'Neal, let's be a'stridin' out."

Across a meadow spangled with a few mountain flowers and bucking a northwest wind angling at them, the horse gaunted some and stepping between the two men, they went at a faster gait set by Finney. Now that autumn was fading away, the sun rode lower in the southern sky. Some distance to the south, perhaps three miles away, there seemed to be a gap through which they could descend along a draw. They began traversing that way over rock-stubbled terrain, the lengths of chain trailing from Finney's legs tinkling metalically on the rocks, the horse stumbling more and reluctant to go on.

About twenty rods in front of them a copse of birch trees with golden, shimmering leafs dropping away in the crisp autumn air brought a quizzical glance from Finney. He could smell danger, and he held up a warning hand. The horse seemed to catch the scent too, and fear began rippling the corded muscles under the dark brown hide as it rolled a wild cerulean eye toward the stand of trees while stamping a foreleg.

"Frank, we'd best get down amongst these rocks."

But the frenzied roar of a bear caught them out in the open, then popping at a dead run out of the trees came a silver-tip. As Frank O'Neal took aim at the approaching bear, the horse reared sideways and slammed into him, flinging O'Neal backwards and down on a mossy green boulder. The lamed horse broke away and eastward, and around thirty futile yards further, the silver-tip, which had changed course, leaped up and sank its clawed forepaws and fanged teeth into the horse's neck, spurting out blood and hunks of flesh.

Finney lunged for the rifle dropped by O'Neal. Turning to O'Neal, he hoisted the man over a brawny shoulder and broke running for the draw. He came onto it just as the agonizing neigh of the horse was cut off with a cruel abruptness. Then the toe of one boot stubbed a rotting log, sending both men tumbling down the draw.

O'Neal was still unconscious when Finney, somewhat stunned from the fall, crawled over and retrieved the rifle. All he could do for the moment was to lay there and wait for the silver-tipped grizzly to come after them.

"To get done in by a grizzly after escaping from that mine," he said disgustedly, "is too damnable much." A lower tooth had been dislodged in his fall, and grimacing, he worked the tooth out of its socket and flicked it away. On his forehead there was a blood-beaded gash, which he ignored. All things considered, they'd lucked out, which proved to be the case, when after a long way, the bear didn't show up. Cradling his companion over a shoulder, he started downslope.

Around the middle reaches of the draw he came upon a stream, whereupon he laid O'Neal on a grassy bank. O'Neal's pulse, he found, was strong, but blood caked the back of his skull.

"Well, they say you can't hurt an Irishman by striking him in the head," said Finney, and with concern trebling in his voice. Filling his hat with icy water, he crouched down and poured it slowly over O'Neal's head, to cleanse the wound some and to rouse the man. A second hatful of water dribbling onto O'Neal's face brought some movement, then a sputtering cough as his eyes fluttered open. After a while they managed to focus clearly on Irish Joe Finney hovering anxiously over him.

"Easy, mon," said Finney. "That was a damned close call."

"All I remember is the horse running over me."

"Lucky for us that silver-tip preferred horse meat."

This provoked from Frank O'Neal a laugh, and through it he said, "That bear's got what provisions we had . . . but at least we're still alive." Suddenly both of them were laughing, into the cutting wind because they'd just cheated death. As their laughter ebbed away, Finney helped his companion to his feet, and with an arm around the smaller man's shoulders to steady him, they went down the draw, and in a little while the valley called Ruby began opening up to them.

"Still a far piece down there."

"We'll be there tomorrow for certain."

"Yup, it's all downhill."

"Now if I were a snowball I could roll down there."

"Speaking of snowballs, Mr. O'Neal, that sky yonder has a hard grey tint; it just might snow tonight."

"It is getting a lot colder."

"This draw should come out someplace near Ramshorn Creek. An outlaw hangout called Robbers Roost is down by the creek. But from the looks of us I doubt any owlhooters will try robbin' us."

"We do look kind of gamey at that. I wonder if Tamerlane's still alive?"

"The difference is, he wants to die."

"Maybe that woman'll change his mind."

Huge snowdrops laden with moisture fell upon the Tobacco Roots long after wayfarers O'Neal and Finney had fallen asleep under canopied aspens. Around them they'd gathered branches and foliage to shield away the penetrating wind. The snowstorm came in steadily, with ponderous grey clouds pushing down upon the mountains, a massive front reaching beyond the valleys on either side of the Tobacco Roots.

Irish Joe Finney stirred first, and heaving to a sitting position, he poked a curious eye out through the screening branches and grimaced at the snow build-up, with more snow slanting down. From the keening wail of the wind he reckoned the storm would blow itself out in a day or two. And he let O'Neal slumber on and set about relighting their campfire. Weariness had kept them from taking turns tending to the fire or keeping an eye out for the nightstalkers. He'd discovered among the ashes in the campfire a single tiny coal no bigger than the pinched-out spark of a cigarette. Quickly he set about collecting a bundle of dry tinder which he formed into a ball. Placing that sparking bit of coal in the center of the tinder ball, he began whirling it at arm's length so that the wind could fan the coal into flame. As the tinder ball began smoking and flame glowed in it, Finney placed it upon the campfire and stacked dry wood over it. When he was certain that the fire would take, Finney went over and with rifle in hand set out amongst the trees in search of small game. Some distance from their campfire, he hunkered down and let his eyes adjust to the diminishing light of night. In a little while he spotted a jackrabbit stirring about in the timber.

When he returned to the campsite an anxious Frank O'Neal said, "That shot spooked me awake. But that rabbit was worth waking to, Mr. Finney. And you called it right about snowing; but I didn't expect this much." A couple of strides brought O'Neal to the fringes of the trees where snow lay in deep drifts. "Too bad we dont' have snowshoes."

"This isn't a real norther," commented Finney as he began skinning the jackrabbit. Next he took out the innards, having placed the pelt over a low branch. Cutting the meat into sections, he sharpened some pieces of wood to use as spits. Once the meat was hanging over the campfire, he cleaned the hunting knife by thrusting its blade into a snowbank. "Well, O'Neal, this meat should give us enough nourishment to get to Ramshorn Creek. And outlaws or no, we're heading for the first sign of smoke we sight."

TWENTY

It was worrying time for Thomas Dimsdale and the other vigilantes, and Sheriff Williams and his deputies, saddlebound as they were under a storm-tossed sky shapeless and threatening. The falling snow was a moving curtain through which they had to pass, so they had to hold their horses to a slow canter along the stagecoach road sloping down into the Ruby Valley. Oftentimes the wind would cut away as if they'd ridden behind a wall, and this time it gave them a clear view of the cutoff trail veering northward among the foothills.

"Think we should turn back?"

Gazing studiously at the editor of the *Montana Post,* Sheriff Jim Williams drawled, "This weather'll keep those hardcases under cover."

"English weather was never like this," said Dimsdale. "Sometimes I wonder what keeps me at Virginia City, out here in this . . . wilderness. Not too many people respect nor understand, for that matter, why there must be a newspaper."

"Oh, they've pretty much got the gist of it, Mr. Dimsdale. Consider this, though. For a heap of them it's been an opportunity to seek their fortunes while getting away from the restrictions of home and family. Maybe the printed word, your *Montana Post,* reminded them too much of what they left behind, family, taxes, an orderly way of thinking and living." The starpacker went on to say Dimsdale's *Montana Post* was civilization's conscience, in a way, a sort of church bulletin and town crier. "And what's riling up the outlaws is those paper bullets you've been firing."

"My editorials," Dimsdale said pensively.

"A lawman's just part of things here," went on the sheriff. "My gun against someone else's. You're that wind of change which most out here will fight tooth and nail. They'll probably fight statehood too, and all that comes with it. Gold brought them here—they'll leave when it stops panning out. Or gold is struck elsewhere."

After following the trail for several miles it died out lower in the valley and the horsemen cut over and rode alongside the Stinking Water River. The storm was letting up, and the range of their vision now took in higher elevations on the mountains and bits of sunlight trying to find seams in the clouds, and down in the valley, trees strung along the Beaverhead River. The presence of men more skilled with guns, the sheriff and his deputies, had done away with any talk of turning back.

They splashed across one creek, with a miner named Bristol saying, "I don't figure there's more'n six or

164

seven road agents hanging out at Robbers Roost. Nothing we can't handle."

"Just the same," cautioned the sheriff, "we'll get into position like I told you before moving in."

One of the merchants coughed nervously. "I've never fired a rifle before."

"When you do," muttered another, "make sure it's loaded."

As he rode, Thomas Dimsdale couldn't dislodge from his thoughts the trial of George Ives which had taken place yesterday morning. It had been an open-air affair, a wagon box being used as the judge's bench and another wagon serving as the jury box. Helping to warm the participants of the trial had been a huge log fire. Also, there'd been frequent sojourns to adjacent saloons so no one actually suffered from the cold. He'd estimated there'd been at least a thousand denizens of Alder Gulch on hand to view the proceedings. A half-hour after a verdict was rendered finding Ives guilty of cold-blooded murder, the luckless man was placed on top of a packing crate and a noose secured around his neck. Someone kicked the box away and George Ives made his drop and strangled to death.

It was while watching Ives die that Dimsdale realized his hand and those of the other vigilantes had fastened the hangman's noose. Even though George Ives had committed murder in the first degree, his sudden involvement in this brought the sobering notion to the editor they were one step removed from mob law. "To catch a thief must one send another thief after him?" he'd debated. Reflecting on all of the people who'd been murdered or disappeared, he'd finally concluded that the law in Virginia City had been corrupted by Sheriff Henry Plummer, that now it must be used by the honest folks hereabouts to make the gulch a decent place to live.

Irish Joe Finney staggered through underbrush laden down with O'Neal, whose condition had suddenly taken a turn for the worst. Earlier, O'Neal had complained of feeling giddy and light-headed, which had only confirmed Finney's suspicions the man's skull had been fractured when their horse had thrown O'Neal onto those rocks. As for himself, the mule-skinner was simply playing out. His face and hands were frost-bitten, as the temperature had plunged to around the freezing mark.

"I fear the worst," Finney mumbled as he sank exhausted into the snow with O'Neal. Despite the cold, he was sweating, something that could prove fatal if they were forced to night out here again. "But I can't leave you, Frank." With a wistful shake of his head Finney turned up the unconscious man's coat collar. "You need a sawbones, bad."

It was the rattling of gunfire that stiffened Finney's body, and brought him to his feet. Breaking through the underbrush, he worked his way up a snow-covered bank, and coming to stand on it, glanced down at the ice-impacted waters of Ramshorn Creek before keening his ears toward the west.

"Could be some outlaws attacking a wagon train or stagecoach."

At a wary crouch he worked his way along the creek

166

while levering a shell in the breech of his rifle. He came to where the creek twisted south-westerly and the trees along it thinned out giving Finney a glimpse of chimney smoke linking out over Pete Daly's ranch-house situated at the mouth of Ramshorn Creek, but more commonly known as Robbers Roost. Until recently, it had been one of the stage stations along the way to Bannack. He couldn't see the house as yet or the other buildings or corrals, but he'd bypassed it more than once with his freight wagons. Working his way under willows bending in the wind, he heard someone cry out in pain before glimpsing armed men firing at the ranchsite from behind rocks and trees, and this brought Finney to a puzzled halt.

Crouching among the willows, maybe a quarter of a mile away, it seemed to him those men assaulting the ranchhouse wore clothing a cut better than your run-of-the-mill hardcase.

"A couple of them are breaking out!"

"The rest of you, surrender or we'll set fire to the house!"

"Got one of them!"

"The other one's made it to the creek!"

"We can't chance going after him! All of you, move in on the house!"

And when the man who'd just spoken turned and waved at the others to follow him, Irish Joe Finney saw the badge pinned to the sheepskin, and with Finney recognizing the district sheriff.

And he promptly forgot about the sheriff as movement further west along the creek caught his eye, and undivided attention. Grimly he watched an

167

outlaw, sixgun in hand, come plunging through deep snowbanks in an attempt to escape. Reversing his hold on the rifle, Finney waited in concealment until the outlaw was a few yards away, in his eyes a disdainful glimmer of hope of getting away from the vigilantes. And then the butt of Finney's rifle knifed through cold, mountain air and thudded against the man's head. The hardcase folded quietly.

"You'll still hang, damn you," Finney said viciously.

Pressing westward along the creek, Finney paused when the ranchsite opened up to him. The vigilantes were closing in on Pete Daly's two-storied house with its outside balcony and overhanging roof and racks of elk and deer decorating the log walls. As the front door lurched open and a white flag of truce began waving, Irish Joe struck back to where he'd left Frank O'Neal. Wearily, but with newfound hope surging in him, he picked up his companion and headed for the ranchsite.

The vigilantes had manacled the wrists of their five prisoners with handcuffs and taken them outside and placed them in a cowshed, over which Sheriff Williams' deputies stood watch. At the moment the sheriff and Dimsdale and others were in the house deciding over hot, brackish coffee the necessity of going after the outlaw who'd escaped along the creek.

"He can't get far in this weather."

"Maybe we should just let him freeze to death."

"My sentiments," said Dimsdale, "but we'll go after him. And he'll hang with the others."

One of the deputies thrust the front door open and blurted out, "Sheriff, you'd best come take a look at this."

168

"Trouble?"

"Be a thinkin' it's either a mountain man headin' this way or someone damned tetched in the head." The deputy, followed by the sheriff and vigilantes edging out of the house, surged through a gate in the picket fence. "Yonder he comes."

"Appears to be some recluse?" questioned one of the vigilantes. "And packing someone else."

"Hello the house!" shouted a tiring Irish Joe Finney, and with his teeth gritting when some of the vigilantes pointed their weapons at him.

"Finney, it can't be you?"

"It's me, alright." He strode through the men stepping to circle wonderingly around him and passed through the gate and carried O'Neal into the shabby living room. Gently he lowered O'Neal onto a worn sofa. Straightening up, he turned and said to Sheriff Williams crowding in with the others, "Any rotgut in this place?"

"Check it out," the sheriff said. Duffing his weathered Stetson, he scratched at his forehead with the same hand. "Just where in tarnation you been? Or come from?"

"I say," said the editor, "isn't that Frank O'Neal?"

A whiskey bottle was passed to Finney, who nodded wearily. "And in bad shape. O'Neal saved my bacon up there." He uncorked the bottle, tipped his head back and gulped down the fiery liquid; it was four fingers lighter when he slumped upon a rickety chair. Wiping spillage from his unkempt beard, he gazed at the sheriff. "You bring a sawbones along?"

"Sorry about that, Irish Joe. What happened

169

to O'Neal?"

"Run over by a horse; fractured his skull some."

Thomas Dimsdale said, "We found what was left of your wagon train down in the Gallatin Valley."

"Nightstalkers done it, gents. Took us up to this hidden gold mine. From what I can figure out it's located in Caribou Gulch. Most of my men and others are being held up there. This snowstorm ain't helping matters either, meaning some of them are in such bad shape they might have gone under."

"Tell me more about these nightstalkers—"

"Sheriff, they're a bunch of no-account murderers bossed by Boone Helm. Helm takes orders from that gambler operating out of Virginia City, a sidewinder a'calling himself George Banefield."

"Well I'll be . . . Banefield opened up an account at my store?"

"I've played poker with him—awful damned generous when it comes to buying a round."

"For Banefield and his bunch money ain't no problem. The gold ore we mine is taken by mule train down to Summit City. Processed at that mine in French Gulch. I've found out that a gent named Jason Webster heads up this damnable operation. This was more or less told to me"—he gurgled down some more whiskey—"by a gent callin' himself Ash Tamerlane."

Frowning, the sheriff settled the Stetson over his uncombed black hair and murmured, "Name rings a bell? Yup, two, maybe three summers ago a lawman out of Utah stopped by my office and told me about this Tamerlane searching for those who'd murdered his family."

"Same gent, sheriff. If he was after me, well gents, I'd hightail it pronto for South America or Asia." Finney shook his head, to chase away some of the bone-weariness and to drive home his point. "Even then I'd keep both eyes peeled to my backtrail. Me and O'Neal came across Tamerlane up in the Tobacco Roots. Parted trails there; us to head back here, an' Tamerlane to trail out to that hidden gold mine."

Sheriff Jim Williams rasped out, "I know about where the gulch is situated. Best way to get there is head along the Ruby Valley, then strike mountainward."

One of the vigilantes, a merchandiser of fine clothing, some of which had been imported from Paris, thrust out his parrot-chest and sucked at his protruding lower lip before saying, "I've had occasion to take some of my wares to French Gulch. I simply cannot believe Mr. Jason Webster would have anything to do with these . . . with these outlaws. If indeed, what Finney says is true."

Before Irish Joe Finney could respond a hand clamped down upon his shoulder and another merchant, cigarillo pouring out angry smoke, stepped forward. This was Farouk Masad, three years removed from Syria, and finding that territorial Montana and its mountains weren't all that different from what he'd know before. Short of stature, around five-and-a-half feet tall, but long on savvy when it came to panning out the truth from downright lying, his piercing black eyes swept disdainfully from the other merchant to fix upon the sheriff. Hooking a couple of fingers around the cigarillo to ease it out of his mouth, he told it plain, "Irish Joe's a man of his word. We have no other choice

171

than to go after these unbelievers . . . these outlaws. My steed's saddled outside. We can replenish our supplies here."

"Couldn't have spoken it better, Mr. Masad. How many men we going against?"

"Well, sheriff, at least twenty, maybe more."

"There's my five deputies and you vigilantes. Some of you'll have to take O'Neal, and Finney here back to—"

"Now whoa, Sheriff Williams. I'm a'heading for Caribou Gulch. Just set my rotting carcass on a hoss and give me a long-gun . . . and maybe another bottle of this rotgut. But Finney's a'going!"

"You look awful done in?"

"Fit as a broken fiddle," came back Irish Joe.

"Seems to settle this argument right quickly," smiled the sheriff. "Mr. Louden, since you voiced your opinion that Finney wasn't speaking true, I'm putting you in charge of getting O'Neal and our prisoners back to Virginia City. And you, Mr. Masad—"

The merchant's words came out mixed with tobacco smoke, "I'll be riding alongside my friend Finney."

"Can't argue with that."

"Don't you think," said Thomas Dimsdale, "we should go after that outlaw we saw heading for the creek—"

Easing up from the chair, Finney said, "You'll find that hardcase stretched out along Ramshorn Creek— about a mile distance. Cracked him hard as I could with my rifle, but just the same some of you vigilantes better make tracks over there. Which I reckon we'd best be doing if we want to take advantage of all this here daylight."

"Hard riding should bring us there late tomorrow."

"Two or three days are all the same to me," intoned Finney. "They burned my wagons. Took my men and me. Done whipped and scarred us with chains. And like my pard Masad just said, it's high time we made believers out of those scum."

TWENTY-ONE

Bellied-down on an outcropping Ash Tamerlane studied the mining camp settled in for the night. The side wound troubled him more than he cared to admit, reckoned it was something he could put up with after viewing through his field glasses that muleskinner getting beaten to death. Passing through Utah, there had been some pictures in a newspaper smuggled out of a Reb prisoner-of-war camp. Those Yankee soldiers had the haggard appearance of men simply waiting to die; such as those below in Caribou Gulch.

The storm had delayed Ash's getting here, with the shape and fell of winter enshrouding the Tobacco Roots. Up on the peaks he could detect some barren spots, the rock formations layered and worn from a million or so years of being at the mercy of the elements. Just a tinge of paling red striped the western horizon. The wind moaned constantly, speaking back to a yapping coyote. It was a shade above freezing, would get a lot colder tonight, and for the prisoners huddled around their campfires in the stockade a night of pure misery. You'd think, Ash mused angrily, the nightstalkers would have enough common sense to let their prisoners bed down in the mine. But the milk of human kindness wasn't a hardcase's strong suit. Or it could be that the honcho, Boone Helm, had orders to work these men until they dropped, and of less importance than those mules chomping away in the corrals.

Earlier on, when he'd seen Wyomia and Boone Helm coming out of a cabin and heading toward another, Ash could feel a surge of emotions. And after Helm had left Wyomia alone with George Banefield and made tracks for that log cabin saloon pouring out fiddle music, there had been little hesitation on Wyomia's part about going into the gambler's cabin. Back east, Wyomia's father had been a prominent banker, so perhaps the man had allied himself with the Cartel. This would explain Wyomia's presence out here.

"Wise up," Tamerlane told himself, "a lot can happen in ten years. She probably doesn't even remember you." But, somehow, Ash's heart beat a different message, one which he chose to ignore. Surely she could talk the nightstalkers into seeing the prisoners had decent clothing and a solid roof over their heads. Or had Wyomia steeled herself to this crooked mining operation, and the way these men were suffering.

Tamerlane's intentions were of a twofold nature: to gain access to that dynamite shack, and if he could come across some weapons, to arm the prisoners, who outnumbered the nightstalkers about three to one. Now, as the night unfolded, sullen blackish clouds ghosting below the peaks, moonless and bitterly cold,

176

he checked out the rituals of the five men standing guard duty. The two nightstalkers keeping watch over the stockade seemed more interested in huddling around their campfire, but every so often they'd take a worn pathway passing in front of the stockade, then trudge back to warm up and suck at a bottle of whiskey. Scoping them again, he grimaced at the cruel indifference to everything but their cheap liquor and patch of campfire warding off the night's chill.

One of the nightstalkers stood guard over the mine shaft, to the west about a hundred rods where the gulch wall impacted into the higher reaches of Diamond Mountain. An incessant smoker, the man left a tendril of wind-bent smoke behind on his frequent trips into the mine, there to ward off the chill and maybe indulge in a private drinking bout of his own. A Union Army deserter, Tamerlane knew, because of the gold stripe adorning the dark blue trousers and the habit the man had of field stripping his handrolled smokes.

North of the mine some fifty yards there was a narrow crack in the gulch wall which, Tamerlane suspected, led down toward the Ruby Valley. This niche of game trail wasn't guarded, that being reserved eastward where Caribou Gulch flowed widely to merge with a mountain plateau. There, two nightstalkers of a soberer bent kept watch. The gulch was more boxy than Alder Gulch to the south, its high, rocky walls forming a screening barrier for the crooked work being done here, and sort of muffling the cutting bites of steel chain into yielding flesh.

Easing away from the dropoff edge of the outcropping, Tamerlane moved back amongst boulders and pines to his horse and deposited his field glasses in a saddlebag. His boots he shucked off and donned a pair of mocassins. With his lariat in hand, he came back onto the outcropping. He tied one end of the braided rope to a juniper and tossed the rope to have it come dangling amid the crowns of trees growing on the gulch floor.

Before descending into the gulch he made certain none of the guards had strayed his way, took a final look at the prisoners huddling in their makeshift huts. He went down quickly, using his legs to keep from rolling into the sheer rock wall. Kicking away from the gulch wall, he grasped a high branch and pulled himself closer to a cottonwood and released his grip on the lariat. From there it was a simple matter to clamber down and touch onto the snow-laden ground.

Over by a corral, a horse switched around causing others penned there to stir nervously about. Another horse stamped at the frozen ground before lashing out with a hind leg at a mule that had wandered too close, but it was the cold more than anything which settled the horses down again. And when they did, the shadowy form of Ash Tamerlane padded silently under the rustling trees and came out by the dynamite shack. The door was locked, but he used his hunting knife to gouge away the hasp from its pine-scented boards, and quickly he slipped inside.

The flare of Ash's wooden match revealed weaponry taken from those the nightstalkers had killed or brought here. There were other supplies, canned food staples, boxes of shells, and saddle rigging. The main part of the shack, and where he found stored boxes of dynamite and fuses, was merely a sort of cave dug into the gulch wall. When his match flickered out, he struck another while going over and taking down a coal oil lamp, which he lit. Now he began the dangerous process of attaching fuses to sticks of dynamite, taping a fuse onto a stick and cutting the fuse so it would explode in about five seconds, then to placing the dynamite he'd prepared in a gunny sack.

Next the rifles stacked against the east wall brought Tamerlane over to find them in good working order but lacking shells, which he also found were plentiful. Now, moving outside, the final step in his plan was getting into the stockade. Then the sound of voices pitched in argument caused Tamerlane to glance over at the saloon where a hardcase stood framed in the open doorway, the glow of his cigar when he uttered angry retorts showing the mangy black beard.

"A cigar's just what I need," said Tamerlane as he detoured around some bushes, "to light those fuses." He watched the hardcase reel away from the saloon and head for a cabin, then Ash trotted over and found the side wall.

Coming around the corner the hardcase had just enough time after spotting Tamerlane to stab for his leathered gun before his beer-swollen belly felt the sting of the hunting knife. He folded over to drop at Tamerlane's feet, who retrieved the man's sixgun and found a couple of cigars in a shirt pocket; the cigar the dead man had been gritting between his gaping teeth started to singe his beard. Quickly Tamerlane retraced his steps into the trees and beelined toward the stockade.

The simple expediency of sinking the trunks of trees into the clay ground and tying them together with crossbeams formed the circular stockade, while a log

179

running crosswise and held in wooden brackets formed a lock for the main gate. Lifting this away, Ash eased it to the ground. Still in a crouch, he checked the location of the two guards, who were hunkered close to their campfire and comparing the notches on the worn butts of their hand guns.

"Before this night has passed away," Ash mused silently, "they're gonna wish they'd never ventured up to Caribou Gulch. The same goes for you, Helm, and that gambler, Banefield. And, Wyomia?" At the moment she seemed like a mystical goddess to him, still graced with a full-bodied carriage and that flowing hair he'd caressed before. But still she was up here where he meant to take his vengeance. Turning elusively as a shadow spun away by an intruding light, he opened the gate just enough to slip into the stockade.

Back where the stockade thrust against the overhanging gulch wall, other logs had been embedded at a downward angle and sealed off with barbed wire. The dirt floor of the stockade had been worn hard by its occupants, huddled inside the flimsy huts or around campfires. The stench of despair and death clung to Tamerlane's nostrils as he crossed toward one of the fires in quest of one of Irish Joe Finney's muleskinners. In the harsh light he grimaced at the ragged clothing of the men lurking there, and at those damning leg irons. Out of eyes sunken deep into their sockets, one of the prisoners gazed bitterly Tamerlane's way.

"Damn you, you come to chain me or someone else to death! Or is it back into the mine we're going tonight?"

Drawing up so that firelight splayed across his face, Tamerlane said, "I'm not one of them."

"Maybe he came to preach us a sermon?"

"Did any of you work for Irish Joe Finney?"

"I'm one of his men. You do him in? or maybe that sonofabitchin' Boone Helm?"

"Finney is still alive," he said quickly. "I came across Irish Joe about three days ago now. I'm hoping by now he's back in Virginia City."

"So you say!" A large, sparse man started to push to his feet. "I've had enough of your lying mouth—"

The man who'd identified himself as being a muleskinner barked, "Let it lay, Willard. Okay, mister, speak your piece—" His name was Thaddeus Mitchem, and a reddish lump swelled on his right cheekbone, but a sudden spark of hope shone in his eyes.

"Obliged," Ash replied. "These nightstalkers ran this same kind of operation down in Colorado."

"So?" spat out the man called Willard.

Unbutting his sheepskin, Tamerlane opened his woolen shirt. Slowly, their eyes going from the scars adorning Tamerlane's chest to his face, all of them seemed to let a piece of what had been happening to them drop away, as Ash said gently, "I've been marred by a chain too. These men murdered my family. Name's Ash Tamerlane."

"How many men you bring, Tamerlane?"

"I came alone."

"Then you came to die!"

Ash squinted up at patches of snow clinging to the dark wall of the gulch. Over the shrilling wind he said, "You men won't last long in weather like this; and it's only going to get worse. I doubt if I'll have any trouble getting out of here and back to my horse. But chained like that, you men won't last long in these mountains.

181

Could be that you men want to die."

"Not me, dammit," said Mitchem. "But your lone gun won't stand a chance against those heathen outlaws."

Tamerlane allowed a smile to trickle across his face. "I gather that none of you are allowed in the dynamite shack?"

"They tote it to us over to the mine."

"I just came from there. Found a lot of dynamite . . . and guns and food. How many are held prisoner here?"

"Name's Thaddeus Mitchem. Around sixty or so, I reckon."

"Okay, Thaddeus, I want you to pick out around ten men." Others had began to drift over in a shuffling walk and bent some, with one or two leaning on the shoulders of a comrade. "You others, tell everyone to settle down."

"You fixin' on gettin' us some guns, mister?"

"Yup. But first we have to get out of here without being spotted." He turned away from the campfire as Thaddeus Mitchem came back with several other men, and Tamerlane led them over to the closed gate. "Thaddeus, once we're outside, angle your men to the southeast amongst the trees. I'll linger behind to barricade the gate again."

He went out first, then the prisoners in a cautious shuffling walk to prevent the leg irons they were saddled with from making any noise. Once he'd replaced the log, Tamerlane took them directly to the dynamite shack. Crowding inside behind the others, he said, "Load as many rifles as you can tote; and take extra shells along. Over there you'll find some spare clothing."

182

"Hey, look, a woolen coat."

"And . . . and blankets! Those miserable bastards would rather we freeze to death than let us have these."

Tugging at Thaddeus Mitchem's arm, Ash led the man aside. "You shouldn't have any trouble getting back into the stockade. There's just those two guards—but they've been boozing it up." Leaning over, Ash picked up the gunny sack containing the dynamite sticks. "When all hell breaks loose, Thaddeus, you and the others make a break for it."

"I figure you got dynamite in that sack."

"You figure right."

"Know how to handle it? I could just go with you, Tamerlane."

"I appreciate that. Who's got the key to those leg irons?"

"Nobody else but Helm. Man just loves to put these damned irons on a person. Save his rotten hide for me." He threw Tamerlane a searching look. "About the only place we can hole up is in the mine shaft."

"Don't try to gun it out with the nightstalkers. 'Cause they're all sharpshooters. I'm just hoping now that Irish Joe is bringing back some help. We could lay low until then—"

"Some of those men back there might not last that long, Tamerlane. We got no other choice but to make a go of it now."

"Just so you understand what you're up against."

"You're the one who's gonna try and take 'em all on. We owe them too."

"First, though, you'd best get your men back into the stockade."

Out in front of the dynamite shack, Tamerlane

183

waited until the prisoners laden with rifles were gone, and until he was reasonably certain they'd made it back into the stockade. Then, reaching for one of the cigars he'd taken from that nightstalker, he drifted the opposite way, the gunny sack slung over a shoulder, teeth gritted around the unlighted cigar, eyes picking out the log cabin occupied by the gambler Banefield and Wyomia Blair.

TWENTY-TWO

The vigilantes cut eastward across the Ruby where it bottlenecked toward the Jefferson River. From the coat-seeking chill of early morning it had warmed considerable, the afternoon sun pouring out liquid heat causing a lot of snow to melt and bring angry water boiling out of the creeks lancing down the mountainsides. Through the foothills they were forced to walk their horses, and with shod hoofs throwing up clods of dirt, come up to a break in a sandstone ridge and a canyon that Sheriff Williams reckoned would carry them up to Caribou Gulch.

"It isn't going to get any easier," was the sheriff's wry comment. "Some of you merchants might have trouble getting your horses up there." His eyes swung from the canyon they would have to climb to the men behind him.

The editor, after swinging to the ground, said, "It hasn't been all that easy getting this far. I'm going on. But we won't hold it against those wanting to turn back."

185

A couple of merchants traded uneasy glances, and finally one of them mumbled, "I believe I will . . . call it quits. Jensen?"

"Same here, I guess. Tracking down outlaws in Alder Gulch is about all I bargained for. Well, good luck to you men."

Silently the other vigilantes watched the merchants swing their mounts around and spur away, and rubbing at his right shoulder to get some of the ache out of it, Irish Joe Finney said, "Can't blame them, I reckon. That leaves eleven of us. And you know"—a smile crackled in his squinting eyes—"that canyon don't look all that steep. It'll be slicker than bear grease though."

Thomas Dimsdale wiped a rivulet of sweat away from his crinkled brow. As had the others, he'd doffed his coat sometime that morning. His dark brown suit was rumpled and sweat-stained and mud seeped around the bottoms of his patent-leather boots. But any discomfort he felt over the miles behind or the climb still to come was forgotten in the urgency of the moment. Those two merchants striking back for Virginia City seemed to take away any uncertainties felt by the others as Irish Joe pointed out a wide level spot shielded by pines some distance up the canyon.

"We should get that far by sundown."

"Barring accidents we should."

"What then, wait there until first light?"

"I say we go on," broke in Finney. "Night's the only time I saw the layout up there. Another thing, if we come up tomorrow when the prisoners are down in the mine, it just might be that Boone Helm'll tell his men to blow up the mine shaft."

"Tonight, then," agreed the sheriff. Placing the cigarette he'd just rolled between his lips. He struck a match to light it against his round belt buckle, and with the scent of his Mex tobacco flaring back to those behind him, Sheriff Williams headed upslope at a slow canter.

Deep in the climbing recesses of the canyon the roar of rushing water came strong to their left, and they got glimpses of the creek as they led their horses upward. A magpie started chattering at them from the screening branches of an aspen. The sun came hot at their backs, and on the vague track there were cracks down which trickled water from the melting snow, this, mingled with the pungent scent of pine. Once in a while one of the vigilantes would slump down gasping, and near spent. Some of their horses weren't faring much better, grain-fed mounts rented out by local livery stables.

"Another half mile and we'll make camp," said the sheriff where he strode out front with Finney.

"Damn," gasped a merchant, "it didn't look all this hard down below."

"I'm winded too," spoke another. "But just thinking of what those men up there have been going through riles my blood."

"We all feel that way," said Dimsdale. And along with others who'd stopped for a breather he struggled upward again.

Without warning, a horse stumbled on the treacherous and wet ground, and in its fear reared sideways as it tried to turn back. There was the sharp agaonizing crack of a bone breaking when its shod hoof came down upon a razored boulder. Whickering in pain, the horse lunged downward to go tumbling into thick

187

brush, to struggle piteously in its efforts to regain its feet.

Handing the reins of his horse to a deputy, the sheriff worked down-slope to the merchant gaping at his suffering horse, and palming his handgun, Sheriff Williams said gravely, "We can't leave it like that."

"A risk we'll have to take," another deputy agreed.

Moving toward the thicket, the sheriff brought his gun to bear on the horse's head and squeezed the trigger, the rippling echo of the shot filling the canyon before fading away. The men eyed one another, certain that now the nightstalkers were aware of their presence. They moved on, glancing more frequently at the jagged mouth of the canyon looming below rock walls stretching toward the darkening sky.

They made camp under trees taking them out of a wind starting to get the bite of winter in it again and the last few seeking rays of a reddish sun fast sinking below Mount Torrey in the Pioneers westward. A suggestion by the sheriff they loosen saddle cinches, and that a couple of his deputies gather firewood, brought everyone into motion along with a questioning glance from Thomas Dimsdale.

"Don't fret now, it'll be a smokeless fire," said Finney. "And shielded by these trees. Sweating during the day ain't healthy for anyone traveling in these mountains."

"Yes, I really feel the chill."

"Anyway," Finney said around an encouraging smile, "I crave some hot java and vittles."

"Do you think they heard that shot?"

"Windy as it is I doubt it."

"You're right, I suppose."

After tending to their horses, the men settled down around the campfire, smoking or exchanging small talk, and savoring the heat coming to dry out their clothing. They'd donned outer garments. Deputy Crandall, claiming to have cooked for a brief spell for the Flying A spread just north of Red Bluff, was slicing bacon from a slab and tossing the strips into a fire-blackened frying pan squatting on burning firewood, the big blackened coffee pot dangling from a wooden spit, while utilizing his hunting knife another deputy was cutting open cans of pork and beans.

Then it was the editor, perhaps out of journalistic curiosity, who inquired about Ash Tamerlane, whether Finney believed the man had reached Caribou Gulch or had perished in the Tobacco Roots.

"He seemed determined enough, Tamerlane did." Hawking tobacco juice down between his legs, Finney added, "Too bad he couldn't wait for us."

Sheriff Williams said, "The thirst for vengence makes a man do strange things. Distorts his common sense."

"The vittles is ready," announced Deputy Crandall. "Fetch your plates and cups and set to it."

Coming anxiously out of the canyon into the pine forest of a high plateau, the vigilantes climbed aboard their horses to follow Irish Joe taking the point. His arduous trek through the Tobacco Roots, and later to be burdened down with Frank O'Neal, couldn't have been accomplished by a lesser man. Only dogged determination had kept Finney saddlebound, and now that Caribou Gulch was just a mile or so away, a new source of energy surged through him, and he rode a little straighter in the saddle. Every so often the moon would appear over his right shoulder to edge back the night. The voice of Sheriff Williams brought Finney glancing the opposite way.

"I've a gut feeling these outlaws don't know we're up here."

"Could be you're right, sheriff. I hope we headed up the right canyon."

"That we'll find out before too long."

"Figure I can pick up that game trail leading down into the gulch. There's Diamond Peak poking up to our right; and that notch where that game trail is located sets just about dead ahead."

"Will we be able to ride our horses up it?"

"Don't rightly reckon so."

Which proved Irish Joe right when the rugged mountainscape through which they were venturing began sagging upward into a bouldery, rock wall, and Finney called out they would have to leave their horses here. Grumbles came from one or two, then as the others were doing, checked the loads in their weapons, and trailed after Finney and Sheriff Williams and his deputies. Since the trail was nothing more than a shoulder-width track taken by wild game down into Caribou Gulch, oftentimes the men would brush against a tree or stumble into underbrush. There was still that fear among a few of their walking into an ambush. When the trail levelled off and those out front could see distant peaks shimmering under moonlight, it was with the realization they were closing on the gulch.

Then, Finney and the deputy striding alongside

pulled up at the unexpected thunderclap of an explosion and a burst of fiery light shoving back the sky over Caribou Gulch. This was immediately followed by another explosion.

Finney spat out worriedly, "It's either Tamerlane having a go of it with the nightstalkers or the prisoners. Let's make tracks down there!"

TWENTY-THREE

Once again George Banefield murmured apologies to Wyomia as he rose from the table and crossed to a gramaphone perched on a side table under the south window. Cranking the handle, the melodious and somewhat scratchy notes of a popular song called "Green Grow the Lilacs" brought a distasteful grimace from Wyomia.

The conversation during a lengthy meal of fried steak and greens and imported wine had been mostly one-sided, the gambler making apologies to Wyomia for the way she'd been brought here, along with Banefield's disclaimers that the ghastly deed had been done by Boone Helm without his knowledge. But between them still lay this bridge of distrust. Damn, how he wanted to bed this beautiful woman, to have her surrender willingly to him. After all, he was on the verge of becoming a very wealthy man. Sitting down again, he gestured toward her empty wine glass.

"I know you'd much rather be at Delmonico's . . . or the Ritz. Circumstances dictate otherwise, I'm afraid."

"I've been told you're a gambler," she said. "Rather a bad one at that. Just how did you get mixed up in this?"

"From an insult to a question," responded Banefield. "You're rather lovely when your temper shows, Mrs. Blair. Let's discuss your presence out here, shall we." He filled her glass, and his, and removing a cigar from a shirt pocket he bit the end away. "You came out west seeking your long, lost lover . . . this Ash Tamerlane. What was it that drove him away in the first place, a lover's quarrel . . . yes, that must be it."

"Yes," she said candidly, "We disagreed about certain things. Just as you mentioned your quitting medical school. What happened, Mr. Banefield, did they find you making love to a cadaver?"

"Damn you!" Before he could stop them the words had jumped out of his mouth. His face became ugly, and he wagged a warning finger at her. "To be defiant is one thing, Mrs. Blair—insulting someone who's trying to help you is quite another matter."

"You kidnapped me, remember!"

"Correction, Wyomia. Boone Helm's men brought you here. And by order of Jason Webster."

"Webster? He's a business acquaintance of my father. What does he have to do with this?"

"Up until now, everything," he said impatiently. Now the gambler's eyes lidded over to hide from her the sudden release of passion, and of arrogance, for wasn't he master of the riches out here in Caribou Gulch. Lowering his cigar to the plate, he shoved his chair away and stepped around the table to grab Wyomia's arm and pulled her to her feet. Hungrily he wrapped an arm around her protesting shoulders and sought Wyomia's full red lips.

"No . . . no—"

"Out here there's nobody to tell me no!"

She clawed at his face to draw blood and managed to pull away.

Enraged, he came at her again, clutching for a shoulder and ripping away her blouse to expose creamy flesh above the form-fitting chemise. She staggered back against the door with a frantic hand groping for the latch. Somehow Wyomia opened the door.

Only to have one of the cabins erupt into flame and seem to come apart before their disbelieving eyes. And he cried out, "It's the saloon!" Lunging forward, he grabbed her by the hair just as someone came their way at a crouched run, a tall man with a cigar clamped between his teeth and reaching to take something out of a gunny sack, the flaring light from the burning cabin revealing who he was to Wyomia Blair.

"Ash?" She shouted desperately. For the briefest of moments they gazed at one another, and then gunfire coming from the nightstalkers drove Ash Tamerlane away. "Ash . . . don't leave me—"

"Kill him!" raged George Banefield as he slammed his clenched fist alongside Wyomia's jawline. "Dammit, kill him!" Then he realized the woman had dropped at his feet, and picking her up, he carried Wyomia back into his cabin to lay her upon a settee. Stepping over, he grabbed one of the rifles out of a gun rack and doused the coal oil lamp as he went outside.

Touching flame to the fuse, Ash Tamerlane tossed the stick of dynamite in the general direction of several outlaws pouring out of a cabin. One of them shouted a warning when he spotted the glowing object coming his way, and they scattered, firing at Tamerlane as the dynamite exploded to tear away part of the cabin and send a couple of nightstalkers reeling to the ground.

Palming the Deane-Adams, Tamerlane fired back at muzzle blasts belching out blue smoke, and spun westward to run along the gulch floor. A sudden spasm of gunfire coming from the stockade brought this from Tamerlane, "Hope they make it to the mine."

"What now, Boone?"

"Spread out!" the outlaw leader shouted back.

"Helm?" questioned Tamerlane, thinking the man had gone down when the saloon was blown apart. And he'd seen Wyomia, her blouse ripped away and lovelier than ever, but with that gambler, and a part of Ash Tamerlane seemed to wither.

"Over here!" a nightstalker shouted upon spying Tamerlane breaking toward some trees. As leaden slugs fanned the air about him, Tamerlane leaped headlong into thorny underbrush, and then to roll away and seek lower ground.

Pressing the glowing end of the cigar to another fuse, he launched the stick of dynamite to hold back those pursuing him, and when it exploded, he made a break for rocks littering a slope just this side of the stockade.

"Tamerlane!"

Recognizing it to be muleskinner Thaddeus Mitchem, he yelled back, "You're supposed to be trying for the mine shaft."

Then the muleskinner came trotting out of the darkness as did several other men clutching weapons, and with Mitchem saying, "You saved our bacon,

Tamerlane. Just returning the favor."

"Some of our men are still back in the stockade, the few that ain't too healthy."

"Yeah, I damnwell know what a chain can do."

"So, Tamerlane, how's it gonna be?"

"Here's how I figure it. There's grub and warm clothing stored in the dynamite shack. Which is where I want you to bring those who aren't armed. It won't be too long before Boone Helm and that gambler figure that whoever controls the weapons still in there is gonna come out top gun in this shootout."

"Won't," muttered Mitchem as he squinted eastward to the lightening horizon, "be too long before dawning."

Another prisoner ventured this, "Them outlaws could just take the horses and mules and skedaddle out of here."

"There's too much at stake."

"Yup, that damned gold," Thaddeus said bitterly. "Okay, boys, let's set up a detail. Carson, take about five men and fetch those still holing up at the stockade over to the dynamite shack."

With the others trotting alongside, Ash Tamerlane brought them to the humping terrain around the dynamite shack, and quickly the men picked out firing positions behind rocks or fallen trees. Occasionally there'd be the report of a handgun or rifle as a nightstalker fired in an attempt to flush out Tamerlane, along with cursing shouts from the outlaws or Boone Helm. What troubled Ash more than anything was that sunup would bring the marksmanship of the night-stalkers into play. Under a mile a man with a Winchester could put a slug into the heart of a running deer or antelope. Studying the terrain, he knew that

197

sooner or later Boone Helm would dispatch some of his men along rimrock.

Slumped next to Tamerlane, Thaddeus Mitchem said, "Guess I'm worried same as you. Just maybe Irish Joe made it back to Virginia City."

"Hope so, Thaddeus. But we can't bank none on that." They fell silent as the other prisoners trickled by to hurry into the dynamite shack.

"Another thing," Ash went on. "We could try hoofing it on foot over that game trail just west of the mine. But with those leg irons your men won't get far."

"Boone Helm's got the only key to these damned things," retorted Mitchem. "Nothing he enjoys more than a-fixing these leg irons to a new prisoner and sending the poor soul down in to the mine . . . but a'whipping him first to drive the spunk out of him. Helm's an inhuman monster. All of us want a crack at him."

"Too bad we couldn't have gotten to the horses."

"They'll be watching them now, for damned certain."

"Well, Thaddeus, it won't be too much longer before they find out the stockade is empty and we're over here. Got enough ammo?"

"Can always use more."

"Take a couple of your men and fetch me some too. And, another thing, I hope my coming here doesn't do us all in."

"Tamerlane, the Good Lord sent you here. And I figure His divine providence is a-seeing to it that help is on the way."

Putting aside his reasons for coming here to Caribou Gulch, Ash Tamerlane stared down at the glowing tip of the cigar he held in his left hand and formed

198

thoughts of Wyomia Blair, sort of sifting out how he felt about the woman. From what he'd seen tonight, it was probably for the best he shy away from thinking of her. Maybe she was the gambler's mistress. Or, a member of the Cartel, and as such, equally guilty for what had happened to his family and all the others made to suffer in this mad pursuit of gold ore.

"Damn, though, she'd still beautiful."

A pensive smile spreading across his face, he spun the image of her away when the shouts of the nightstalkers came westward from the stockade.

TWENTY-FOUR

"The prisoners have escaped!"

"Killed two of our men."

His eyes blazing cold anger, Boone Helm said, "Tamerlane and the others are probably holed up in the mine. Which suits me fine. You two, get some dynamite."

"Dammit, Boone," said George Banefield, "We can't blow up the mine shaft. Man, we're this close to hitting the mother lode."

"That sonofabitch Tamerlane killed some of my men and tried to do me in over at the saloon. I want him dead, no matter what."

Swinging his rifle to cover Helm, the gambler said, "You fool, that gold is ours now. Think on it, man, with it you'll live like a king for the rest of your life. In any country you like. We need those prisoners. Later you can rip out Tamerlane's heart for all I care, Boone."

"You're sayin' that because of the woman," sneered Boone Helm. "Alright, hold off with that dynamite. Check out the mine."

"What if they ain't in there?"

"Do it!" Helm exploded. There was still burning in him a need to strike back at the gambler for insulting him in front of his men, a man he didn't respect, nor like. But what Banefield had just said took the edge from his bloodletting mood. To keep the prisoners alive just long enough for them to locate the mother lode—after that, they died, as would the gambler.

He gazed through eyes made bloodshot from drinking to the sky becoming lighter above the encroaching walls of the gulch, and aware also that he and his made a tempting target standing as they were in front of the stockade. Sourly he told them to spread out more. A few minutes later those he'd sent to the mine returned.

"The shaft is empty."

Helm swore viciously. "They broke into the dynamite shack. Holed up someplace near it."

"They could be making a try for the horses—"

"We got men watching the corrals. Half of you go with Banefield . . . and circle to come in from the north and east. Curly, pick out a couple of men and get them buffer rifles. Then work your way up yonder along the north rim."

"This'll be a turkey shoot."

"Hold your fire until I locate Tamerlane. Like the gambler told us, we need them prisoners to get at that gold ore. Now move, dammit!" With an eager grimace for those still with him, Boone Helm checked out the loads in his rifle as he moved purposely away from the stockade. Eagerly he looked ahead to killing some of the prisoners, chiefly to teach them a lesson. Afterwards, when he'd killed the gambler, that woman would share

202

his bed. And even as the men with him were spreading out into a skirmish line, the outlaw was pondering over ways to discard them after he'd secured the gold.

The vigilantes came to bunch along the game trail wending down into Caribou Gulch and stare at the havoc caused by Ash Tamerlane. It was Irish Joe Finney pointing out the stockade, the mine shaft, beyond that the various cabins and corrals. Flames still poured from burning buildings reddening the clearing sky. But Irish Joe's concern was for the nightstalkers fanning out as they began to encircle those waiting for them by the dynamite shack.

"Coming onto daylight," mused the sheriff. "That ground mist floating near the gulch floor is going to be a problem. It'll be like gunning away in a dark room . . . and no telling who we'll hit."

"I've been counting heads," said Dimsdale. "There seems to be around twenty to thirty outlaws, not counting those lurking around the corrals."

Finney gestured at three men who suddenly materialized out of the shadows below and were working their way up the north wall of the gulch. "Those hombres are toting buffalo rifles. One slug from them guns will tear a man's head right off."

"I say we do to them," piped up the merchant Farouk Masad, "what they plan to do to the prisoners. First we do away with those outlaws climbing up that wall—"

". . . and commandeer those buffer guns and give the nightstalkers a taste of their own medicine."

"For certain we'll have those outlaws in a crossfire," grinned Finney. "Okay with you, sheriff?"

Plucking a leaf from a limb of the quaking aspen under which he stood, Sheriff Williams nodded agreement and looked northward to study the gulch wall. There seemed to be, several yards just below rimrock, a long rocky shelf toward which the outlaws were climbing.

"I'll push on ahead with my deputies," he said. "Trail in behind and wait until you hear the call of an owl."

"Just hope we don't mistake it for the real thing."

"You won't," the sheriff replied as he brought his men out from under the trees. Hurriedly they struggled over bouldery ground to finally swing to the east but keeping back from the gulch wall.

Sparodic gunfire came from Caribou Gulch as Finney and the vigilantes, wearied from coming on foot up here, and having been up all night, started after the sheriff and his deputies. But there were no mutterings of complaint, just a shared notion that in a little while some of them could be dead.

"It is Allah's blessings, Irish Joe, that we are here."

He gazed at the merchant Farouk Masad trying to match his longer stride, and then he drawled, "Maybe so. But them heathen nightstalkers don't cater to any religion. Had any experience handling a rifle?"

"Violence is common to my country, also."

Both of them, the others, glanced canyonward when guns began hammering with a killing vengence, and with the editor murmuring, "Your men are giving those outlaws more than they can handle."

"Just hope they save some for me."

Approaching the place where they'd spotted the three outlaws bringing up those buffalo guns, but deep among trees growing on the sloppy terrain, Finney's

204

upraised arm halted the vigilantes, and some of them slumped down on the ground or rocks. Finney, starting to limp himself, said, "A shame we don't have any of the Devil's brew along. This mountain water's startin' to rust my pipes." His quiet laughter produced some hesitant smiles, with their faces sobering and ears keening to the eerie call of an owl.

"Single file from here on," said Finney. With the muscles in his left leg starting to knot up, he limped ahead of the vigilantes, and suddenly the tip of the sun struck out as bright as a cannon's flare from behind a distant peak to temporarily blind Finney. But he blinked the sudden light out of his eyes and kept moving toward the upper reaches of the gulch, commenting to nobody in particular, "Morning sure has a way of bushwhacking a man."

Beyond the muted aspens Finney could see down into the gulch, and motioning for those with him to spread out, he went on alone at a crouch. From there he crawled to the crumbling edge of the high wall and gazed down where Sheriff Williams and his deputies were sprawled on a wide ledge. Trussed up nearby were the three nightstalkers.

"It's still a little hazy down below."

The sheriff replied, "We'll wait until the sun clears more before seeing how good these buffalo guns are."

"Just save Boone Helm for me."

TWENTY-FIVE

It didn't take long for Tamerlane to realize the men closing in on them were marksmen who were using the screening trees and rocky terrain to work ever closer. Though he'd nicked one or two of them, men more accustomed to muleskinning and pounding rocks were firing wildly, and mostly at shadows. Just to his left under an elm tree a muleskinner lay humped over dead. In the windless air hung the stench of spent gunpowder.

"Make your shots count!" he yelled out. He'd swapped the Deane-Adams for a Winchester. Snapping off a slug at the evasive brim of a hat, he sprang up and ran westward to see how the prisoners entrenched amid a rockpile were faring.

"You don't jerk that trigger; squeeze it gently. And the next time you spot someone breaking for new cover lead him some."

"Can't see much in this fog."

"Neither can the nightstalkers." A bullet snapped into a rock close to Tamerlane's head and ricocheted away; he flinched at the stinging pain of some rocky chips.

"What do you think of our chances?"

"We're making our chances," he said encouragingly. With a hasty smile for the bearded muleskinner, Ash crouched away and then broke running back to sprawl alongside Thaddeus Mitchem, who'd sustained a flesh wound to his left shoulder.

"Got careless," he said around a digusted grimace. "Had a chain dig in deeper'n this."

"These outlaws know their business."

"You got something in mind?"

"Maybe I'm hoping they'll run out of ammunition. Praying too, Thaddeus, that help arrives."

Until the ground mist had cleared away, the nightstalkers could only hold their positions and exchange fire with Tamerlane's men. And those three men up on that rocky ledge, pondered Boone Helm, could pick off anyone making a break for the livestock. He beckoned a hardcase to his side, told the man to fetch those watching the corrals. As the hardcase sprinted away, Helm cast cold and dispassionate at one of his men sprawled lifeless over a rock. Treating people kindly wasn't in Boone Helm's makeup. Impatiently he called out, "Curly, just beyond this meadow there's a rise looking down on that dynamite shack. I want you and Jim Bob to hightail it over there."

"Hell, Boone," muttered the Texan, the one called Jim Bob, "Traversing across that meadow'll put us right under their guns."

"We'll pin them down with covering fire. Now, get to it!" His clothes were singed from having to tumble out the back door of the saloon a split-second before that dynamite had exploded. Anger still simmered in Helm from that, and now at the obvious cowardice of this Texan.

"Maybe Curly here'll go for it—but not me, Boone."

Without hesitating the outlaw leader angled the barrel of his Henry at the Texan's midsection and pulled the trigger. Grunting in pain and shock, the impact of the heavy slug driving him sideways, Jim Bob clutched at his belly while doing a little stumbling walk. A second slug belching out of the rifle broke the man's spinal cord. As the Texan nosedived to the ground, Helm whirled on the other outlaw.

"Any questions?"

His face as white as the lifting mist, the nightstalker ran blindly out into the meadow. Droplets of condensed moisture winking in the sun spilled away from bear grass ripping at the nightstalker's pumping legs; then he tripped over a rock and went sprawling. He came up clawing at his gun and with the nightstalkers hammering away at their former prisoners. Then a lone answering shot punched into the outlaw's chest, and he fell out of sight in the tall grass.

"That had to be Tamerlane!" cursed Boone Helm. He shouted for his men to stop firing.

Off to Helm's left and about twenty yards away, the gambler Banefield twisted away from his firing position on the slanting top of a boulder and came hunkering over to say while reloading, "We've got to kill Tamerlane. Which means we've got to get him out into the open so's our men up there with those buffer guns can have a go at him."

Sneering, Helm muttered, "I've tried killing him down in Colorado . . . and up hereabouts. He's just damned lucky."

"Maybe his luck's run out."

"How's that?" Slumping down, Helm removed some slugs from his cartridge belt.

"We use that woman as bait."

Suspiciously the nightstalker stared back at Banefield, and he muttered jeeringly, "Didn't reckon you had the stomach for that kind of work—"

"That gold makes all the difference, Boone."

"I've seen men get killed arguing over two bits. But that gold does set a man to thinking. It's kind of whetted my appetite for the finer things in life. Like that Wyomia dame. Any objections in that?"

"The gold is all I want," lied the gambler.

Fixing a lopsided grin, Helm said, "Guess I've been reading you all wrong. Reckon, too, I'll have to watch my backside more when you're around."

Wyomia Blair sat up groggily to the sound of gunfire. She was surprised to see sunlight streaming in through the windows. Lowering her feet to the floor, she reached up to touch her swollen jawline. Flinching at the sharp pain when she tried to open her mouth, Wyomia rose only to fall back dizzily onto the settee. Steeling herself, she struggled to her feet and moved unsteadily over to the washstand by the open bedroom door and gaze into the shard of mirror above it.

210

Staring at the tangled mass of shoulder-length hair framing her ashen face, a deep anger surfaced to harden Wyomia's eyes, the little touch of mascara and bluish powder in disarray. All of a sudden she remembered Tamerlane's presence. The man she loved had come to set her free, and now the ongoing booming of guns carried her over to throw open the front door.

"Ash must be in trouble?"

"Going someplace," said an approaching George Banefield.

Recoiling from him, she spun around and broke for the lone rifle resting in the gun rack. But the gambler caught her arm just as Wyomia lifted it away. He tore the weapon from her, then sent her tumbling away.

"Damn you," he said through a bitter smile, "I promised you everything."

"I don't want any of your damned gold!"

"Gold," he countered, "is all women like you understand. Gold is power, my lovely. Paris, Rome, you can have all of it. Either you become my woman or Tamerlane dies."

"Never!"

"Never is being dead for all eternity." In spite of the woman's defiance, in her eyes shone Wyomia's love for Ash Tamerlane, and somehow the gambler kept his emotions from showing. He had the man she loved in a vice of certain death. Still, he wanted to inflict pain upon this spirited woman, break her down so she'd come crawling to him.

"Time's running out, Wyomia. For you and Tamerlane. Boone Helm's men are holding off until I come back. Either you obey me from now on, become my woman, or you'll see Tamerlane buried. Then I'll personally take you in chains over to the Chinese cribs in Butte. Once those Chinamen get their hands on you, my lovely, whoring will be all you'll ever know."

"Seems you're holding the better hand, gambler," she said dully. "But remember this, damn you, Tamerlane lives. Because if you have him killed, every waking moment I'm with you will be hell on earth. I'll simply be waiting for that moment when I can kill you."

"You'll change your mind in time," he said cockily. Removing his coat, he draped it over her shoulders. "Sorry I had to tear your blouse." Then he brought Wyomia out of the cabin and past the smoldering remains of the saloon and other cabins Tamerlane had dynamited. Now that a deal had been struck he felt more possessive of her, resented Boone Helm's carnal interest. The man was nothing more or less than a killing machine; there was an eeling of fear at the thought.

Veering onto a worn pathway the nightstalkers used when going to the mine, the sun above the mountains lancing at his back and Wyomia's, the gambler inhaled lustily her lilac-scented perfume. Why hadn't he simply forced his intentions on her last night? Then, clearing a stand of cottonwoods, there were the eyes of Boone Helm telling what he'd do to the woman if given half a chance. He brought her over to Helm squatting behind a screening jumble of rocks and thicket, and with Helm jerking a thumb at the meadow lying between them and Tamerlane and the prisoners.

"Tamerlane gives himself up or you die, hussy!"

"That wasn't the deal, Boone!"

"Take a look around, gambler," jeered Helm.

One of the nightstalkers grabbed Banefield's rifle and shoved him aside, and Banefield blurted out, "I suppose you plan to kill the prisoners too?"

"Nope, since from now on you'll be one of them." He laughed with the others moving in to cluster around their leader. "Just Tamerlane." Rising lithely, Helm wrapped a hand in Wyomia's hair and drew her close so that his whiskey-sour breath, cruel beard-stubbled face, made her cringe away in fear. "Now, hussy, you and me's gonna take a little hike."

He forced Wyomia through the rocks and upon the edges of the meadow, where he shouted, "Tamerlane! You hear me, Tamerlane?"

"Loud and clear!"

"That's better! See what I brung you, Tamerlane? Wyomia, that old hussy you left behind."

"I see her."

"Here's the way of it, Tamerlane—give yourself up or she dies!" He shoved her stumbling further into the meadow, crouched and brought up the Henry to cover her. "Keep walking, hussy!"

When Wyomia Blair saw bushes stirring at the other end of the meadow and Tamerlane appeared, she yelled, "No, Ash! They're going to kill you!"

The unexpected roaring of the buffalo guns caught a lot of nightstalkers out in the open, coming over as they had to watch Helm have his way with the woman. Slugs from the three buffer guns, sounding almost as one, felled three outlaws. Sheriff Williams, who'd decided to rely on his own rifle, punched a hole in another, and from further up along rimrock the vigilantes began firing away.

When the man guarding him swung startled eyes in the direction of those yammering guns, George Banefield stabbed a hand into his shirt for his hideout gun, and whirled to shoot the outlaw in the throat. Oblivious to everything but the way Helm had doublecrossed him, he scrambled over the rocks, and when he saw Boone Helm standing out in the meadow, and the woman down, he snarled, "You damned fool!" He fired to empty his two-shot Derringer, and Helm staggered as the slug found his hip. Then the gambler gasped in shock when a slug from a buffer gun took him high in the back, and he felt no more.

"Let's get them!" came the shout of Ash Tamerlane as he brought those with him in a shambling run hobbled by chains toward their tormentors.

Though the slug had staggered Helm, it had also served to tell him he had to escape. He went limping into aspens, starting to be rippled by a slight wind, and toward the corrals. He left behind the nightstalkers, starting to feel the wind of defeat; already he'd shoved aside any notions of helping them. There'd be other jobs like this, or banks to be robbed or stagecoaches. At one of the corrals, he reached for a lariat coiled over a post, and crouching into the corral, eyed the circling horses before flicking the lariat out to rope a big hammerhead. Hurriedly he saddled the horse, and then Helm was galloping eastward along the gulch floor tapering up to a high plateau.

Leaving the gold behind didn't bother him as much as it had the gambler, but not having his way with the woman did, and he cursed. Only later, when urging the bronc out of the gulch and into the unknown reaches of the Tobacco Roots, did he begin to feel the nagging pain of his hip wound.

Only later did Boone Helm become aware that clinging to his backtrail was a vengeful Ash Tamerlane.

TWENTY-SIX

Going on three days now Tamerlane had clung to the trail of the outlaw, Boone Helm. Behind in Caribou Gulch he had left a terrible carnage, that of the muleskinners and other prisoners either gunning down or, he reckoned by now, hanging the other nightstalkers. He'd glimpsed the body of the gambler, Banefield. And of Wyomia being taken away by Thaddeus Mitchem, so she at least was still alive. Do they hang women out here? Back there she'd shouted out that they were planning to kill him, had it been to save herself?

Ahead, by Tamerlane's reckonings, the outlaw was working his way through another mountain valley. Tamerlane rode warily, and in no particular hurry, since he was pursuing a wounded man, testified to by the few blotches of blood he'd come across. In weapons they were about even, Helm toting that Henry and a handgun, or maybe two. As for the ways of the mountains, it was here that Tamerlane had the decisive edge. And it was all one and the same if this chase went

217

on for a week or more, for in the end Helm was going down. First though, he would narrate to Tamerlane the names of those who murdered his family down in Colorado.

Another day closed, wind-tossed and achingly cold, and for Ash Tamerlane it was a night to be close to the luxury of a campfire. Thus far this had been denied the outlaw, but sooner or later, if not tonight, Boone Helm would get careless and make one of his own. There was even the possibility of Helm's circling back to ambush Tamerlane.

Come dawning, and when this hadn't happened, Ash saddled his horse hobbled by the bank of a meandering creek, and set out again. He was in a small valley near the northern limits of the Tobacco Roots, and as he rode, Tamerlane soon picked up tracks left by the outlaw's horse being forced across a marshy place, and with Ash simply skirting it to pick up the trail beyond.

Upon waking this chilly morning to frost bowing down the limbs of the trees he'd camped under, Tamerlane knew with a deadly certainty there'd be a showdown sometime today. Out of the valley he rode, the slope he was on stippled with Douglas firs, and with golden sunlight striking down through openings amongst the thick green branches. The horse, a bay having a tendency to side-step, perked up its ears, and Tamerlane lifted his right hand away from the Deane-Adams as an elk danced away.

"Easy," he murmured, more for his own ears than for the mount he rode.

On a high ledge Tamerlanc discovered there were two routes open to him, to turn around and strike back down into the valley, or along a sheer rock wall where the ledge formed a hazardous trail to what lay beyond. Dismounting, he slaked his thirst from the canteen. And for a thought still unclear to him, Ash unsheathed his Winchester, while building in him was a wary sense of unrest. The very fact the outlaw hadn't managed to stem the flow of blood coming from his wound told Tamerlane the slug was still lodged in there; and after three relentless days of trying to get away, Boone Helm was looking for a place to make a stand. Gazing ahead at the route he had to traverse, a rod or so wide track passing around a curving mountain wall, displeasure and a lot of anxiety flickered in his eyes. The horse, perhaps catching the scent of the outlaw or his horse, pawed with a shod hoof at the hard, pebbly track.

Tugging at the reins, Ash went ahead of his horse to clear treeline and pass by knee-brushing sagebrush before actually stepping onto the ledge hanging several hundred feet above a mountain lake sparkling in the sun. The ledge stretched northward for about a quarter-of-a-mile, he discovered after being on it for some time, as it ventured underneath the granite wall. Every so often he was forced to work cautiously around fallen rocks and outcroppings in the wall.

"Pow!"

That first bullet from Boone Helm's rifle caught the horse in the belly, and jerking the reins out of Ash's hand, it attempted to rear up, and swung crazily toward the outer edges of the ledge, and suddenly it was whickering downward and beyond Tamerlane's range of vision. Somehow Tamerlane managed to flop down as two quick slugs punched chips out of the wall. Rolling behind a bulge in the wall, he made no attempt to fire back. Twisting to glance back over his shoulder, he knew to make a break that way would see him gunned down by Helm.

By the sun it was closing onto noon, and Ash Tamerlane settled in for a long, thirsty wait. That tactical error of Helm's—going for the horse first—would cost him dearly, Ash pondered. Probing his pockets, he came upon one of those cigars he'd taken from that nightstalker. And patiently Tamerlane dragged smoke from it while waiting for the long, chilly afternoon to run its course.

"Wyomia," he mused, "seems strange that after all this time we encounter one another again." Flooding back, too, came visages of others out of his past: college classmates, that red-haired woman down in Mescalero, that maitre d' at that ritzy Manhattan night club who'd had Ash and several other college friends thrown out for rowdy behavior, those passionate times with Wyomia, remembrances of Africa and family, and finally, that bitter trail he'd followed out here for the past ten years.

Another slug from Helm's long gun, as he'd been doing for most of the afternoon, broke Tamerlane's reveries. He hadn't fired back. But what he regretted as shadows lengthened along the ledge and covered Ash was that his sheepskin had been tied behind his saddle. An eagle winged overhead just as the sun vanished, and during the day he'd watched turkey vultures darting out of the azure-blue sky and sweep below to find the dead horse. During their winged descent he'd also had the feeling they'd marked his position as well.

Patiently he lurked there far beyond sunset, knowing that a man of Helm's impulsive nature would get careless, and a deeper blackness would give him all the cover he needed to clear this ledge. As it had been doing for several nights running, soon the moon would be clearing those peaks to the southwest judging from the presence of a palish light that way.

Now, without thinking too much on it, Ash Tamerlane leaped up from where he'd been sitting with his back braced against the rocky wall and slipped along the ledge in a running crouch. And shortly, slugs from the outlaw's rifle began chipping rock around him. He came off that ledge at a run and carried upward to throw himself onto the lower branches of a limber pine before his weight carried him down onto the loamy ground. Immediately he regained his footing and went on among trees shelfing up to a rocky fortress where the outlaw seemed to be holed up, and with Tamerlane detecting the faint glowing of a campfire.

Working his way upslope just to the west of the campfire, Ash would pause from time to time and listen for any sound made by Boone Helm. A wounded man, he reasoned, wouldn't have the gumption to crawl amongst these jagged and perilous rocks forming a high outcropping, and Ash was proved correct when he spotted a shade of movement just beyond the campfire. In his arrogant conceit at having Tamerlane at his mercy, the outlaw had made a fire, and Helm huddled close to it like a blind man groping along a dark alley.

"Tamerlane!"

Along with uncertainty he'd detected the pain in Helm's brutish voice, and he didn't respond, but lurked there with his Winchester ready for a snap shot, knowing that for Boone Helm it was twilight time.

"Damn you, Tamerlane, don't you want to hear about your family? About how me and my men done them in?"

Piercing the night and Tamerlane's ears came the outlaw's diabolical laughter, and in Ash there was contempt mingled with that terrible anger. He slipped between two boulders to work his way closer.

"Your sister, Tamerlane, had my way with her whilst my men were a-pleasurin' themselves with your ma. Raped her, I did. Then slit her throat. Tamerlane, damn you . . . answer me—"

And Ash Tamerlane did, having slipped closer under cover of darkness, but angling around so's he came at Boone Helm's backside. Cruelly he jabbed the business end of his Winchester into the nape of the man's neck, and said chillingly, "That's right . . . go ahead . . . try me—"

The Henry fell out of Boone Helm's nervous fingers, and Tamerlane kicked it away, jerked the handgun out of its holster, and cast it over the ledge of the outcropping. "Alright, Helm, get up, damn you . . . down by the fire." Now he slapped the man's hat away with his gun barrel to spur him into movement.

"Can't hardly walk," complained Helm as he used his arms and good leg to drag himself up to the campfire. There, firelight revealed to Tamerlane a face twisted in pain and hatred. Laughing, he added, "That got to you, Tamerlane, me a-tellin' you the truth of what happened to your family. So now you'll take out this slug and fetch me back to stand trial. I'll warn you now . . . there's a heap of miles between here and Virginia City . . ."

"Take off that sheepskin!"

"Easy, Tamerlane," whinned the outlaw, and with some reluctance he shrugged out of it and tossed it

Tamerlane's way. "You a-fixin' to freeze me to death."

"Up—and over there!" Struggling upright, Helm gaped with some consternation at the sheer outcropping edge, and back to the other man. "Your kind just don't do this, Tamerlane!"

"My kind don't rape helpless women either!"

Fanning the lever on his Winchester and firing, Ash found himself emptying the rifle at the outlaw, the slugs ripping holes from protruding belly to forehead and driving Boone Helm over the outcropping edge, to have him fall silently out of Tamerlane's life.

His decision to kill the outlaw had been a spur of the moment thing, and in a way it sickened Ash Tamerlane. Slumping down by the fire, he realized for doing it he was no better than Helm or any of his nightstalkers.

"What's happened to me?"

There was still those belonging to the Cartel, with a sadder Ash Tamerlane wanting to call this thing off now but realizing the game must be played out to its deadly conclusion. In his present state of mind he could almost visualize himself gunning down Wyomia. As the bible says, as his father had often versed it to him, he who lives by the gun must die by it. And, there was still the fact of his presence up here amongst these forbidding peaks. Come morning he'd try to find the outlaw's horse and strike back to civilization and what was to come. Retrieving the coat, he donned it and settled into Helm's bedroll, so weary of body and mind that he lapsed into a dreamless sleep.

TWENTY-SEVEN

Once they'd reached St. Louis by following the Missouri to where it confluenced with the Mississippi River, the travelers had little difficulty in selling their horses and saddle rigging to the owner of a drayline business. Boarding an eastbound Union Pacific passenger train, Frank O'Neal and his new wife made themselves comfortable in a Pullman sleeping compartment, to be joined by Ash Tamerlane after they'd gotten underway.

"This calls for a drink," quipped O'Neal, and turning to a bucket of ice reposing on a side table, he plopped cubes into three glasses.

Tamerlane swung his eyes away from Molly O'Neal—that concerned glow for him in her hazel eyes—to gaze out a window where dusk was etching its shadows through the leafless trees which stood forlornly along the right-of-way. Winter had pushed them out of territorial Montana, and upon arriving at Cheyenne, Tamerlane had firmed up his decision not to go the slower stagecoach route to St. Louis, telling the

225

O'Neals he could make better time, and perhaps move ahead of the coming storm clouds by cutting cross-country; much to his surprise they'd agreed with his decision. More of a surprise to Ash had been Frank O'Neal's decision to return to New York. Though the new Mrs. O'Neal had a lot to do with it, there was still in Ash a lingering skepticism, and taking the glass of brandy passed to him, he said, "We're not all that different, Frank."

"How's that?"

"Guess both of us are lawbreakers now."

"I've told you before, Ash, Boone Helm deserved no better'n you gave him. And the outlaws Sheriff Williams jailed down at Bannock will testify to what Helm and those nightstalkers done to your family . . . and also against Jason Webster."

"Perhaps," Ash said despondently. "So you still believe that businessman you blackmailed, Horace Eliot, is mixed up with the Cartel? But if he isn't, Frank, you'll probably wind up in jail."

"He is, I know it," O'Neal said crisply as he eased down next to Molly. "I didn't pick up the connection until you mentioned Webster's name. Knew I'd heard it before. At first I figured it was in the newspapers . . . then when you described Webster to me . . . there it was. I'd seen them buddying-up back in New York . . . at Delmonico's, aye, and other places. So you see, Ash, Molly, it's Providence me blackmailing Eliot and vacationing out in Virginia City."

Molly smiled as he passed an arm around her shoulders. "You have such a splendid way with words."

"Is that the reason you married me, Molly dear."

"Your blarney, and because I just happen to love you."

"This wife of mine, Ash, has a cutting way with words; anyways, I just happen to love her too."

Lowering his glass Tamerlane said, "At least we have two names."

"She'll be back there too, Ash," Molly said gently.

"And all she ever wanted was you, Ash Tamerlane."

"Not anymore, I'm afraid."

Virginia City had still been talking about the return of Irish Joe Finney and others who'd been held captive at that secret gold mine when Tamerlane had ridden in. It was through Frank O'Neal, and of course, Molly, that he'd learned the true reason Wyomia Blair had come a-seeking him, and that there was no connection on her part to Jason Webster's Cartel. But she had recently departed on the Wells Fargo stagecoach for Cheyenne and home again. He had spurned not only her love but her reasons for being out here. Perhaps, Ash had rationalized, there was no longer in him the capacity to love, to care, to settle into a place or relationship with a woman. And it wasn't over yet, despite all the agonizing he'd done over the ruthless way he'd killed Helm, and others. New York and Jason Webster awaited him, and perhaps his own demise, or imprisonment as would probably happen to Frank O'Neal.

Peering at O'Neal over the rim of his glass, it suddenly occurred to Ash that here was a friend, someone siding with him because of friendship—at that moment some of Ash's bitterness shredded away.

"You had a claim on that gold too—"

"In Caribou Gulch?"

"Yup, Ash, as I did. Would have been nice to stampede back there and help dig for that mother lode. And it's there, according to those who'd been forced to work that mine."

"To me all gold has done is bring death . . . and sad times."

"Once this is settled in New York," said Molly, "it's off to California where Frank wants to get back into the detective business."

"You folks deserve that, and more."

"As you do Wyomia."

Through the valleys and towns of midwestern America they rolled, and onward across the night-enshrouded Appalachians. On into eastern New York where a rail network converged at Hoboken and the Hudson Yards and beyond to plunge down the finger of Manhattan to the Battery. Disembarking at last from the passenger train, Tamerlane and Molly O'Neal looked to her husband for direction that would carry them away from the crowd milling about the train station.

"It's barely five in the morning," said O'Neal. "Since the Webster Building is over on Broadway, I suggest we find lodging at the Astor Hotel."

"Suits me," said Ash, as O'Neal flagged down a hansom cab. Once their luggage was stowed and they were settled into the cab, Ash gazed out upon a city he'd known with a youthful intimacy. The sound of it, after a while, got to him, a disembodied, all-prevasive sound of everything seeming to happen at once, along with that closed-in feeling thrown down by the towering buildings. Out in the west a man could almost

228

hear himself musing over that next move, and Ash could also feel his nerves jangling some.

"It'll come back," smiled O'Neal.

"Liking it here?"

"Seems like I've never been gone."

"Seems I'm a stranger in an alien place," Ash commented wryly, removing his Stetson to settle it upon his lap.

During their train journey it had been decided by both men that it would be necessary to enlist the help of a police detective, and for Frank O'Neal this meant Detective-Lieutenant Shawn Muldoon, the man heading up the bunco squad. At the Astor Hotel, a uniformed doorman snapped his fingers and quickly there appeared bellhops to take charge of the newcomers and their luggage.

"Get your *New York Times* here!" yelled a passing newspaper boy.

"At last, civilization," said O'Neal as he flipped the lad a nickel and was handed a newspaper, which he folded and tucked under one arm and trailed the others into a spacious lobby.

Upstairs in his suite, and with Ash Tamerlane going to another room across the hallway, Frank O'Neal tipped the bellboy and requested he bring back some coffee and sweet rolls. After the bellboy had closed the door, O'Neal turned and smiled at his wife checking her appearance in a wall mirror. "Tired?"

"Mostly worried."

"Molly, it'll be alright—and anyway, you wanted this too." Unfolding the newspaper as he eased tiredly onto an overstuffed davenport, he looked at the front page, and there it was; toward the lower portion of the

229

page, a copule of columns devoted to the man they were after, Jason Webster.

"I'll be . . . damned! Molly, he's dead."

"Whatever are you talking about?" But turning away from the mirror, she found her husband leaving their suite and crossing the wide hallway to pound on the door leading into Tamerlane's room.

"It's open."

Shouldering into the room, O'Neal said bitterly, "Guess we'll be attending Mr. Webster's funeral instead." He handed the newspaper to Ash.

The only change in Ash Tamerlane when he scanned the article was a slight narrowing of eyes and the tightening of jawline muscles. Dropping the newspaper on the bed, he reached to pick up his Stetson, and then glanced coldly at the Irishman.

"Believe I'll go for a walk," he uttered distantly, and he went away.

Aimlessly an angry Ash Tamerlane walked the streets, catching the curious glances of people not accustomed to western garb, but seemingly unaware of this, sunken as he was in a deep well of bitterness and frustration. He strode through Washington Square and came onto a street angling off to the southeast until a pagoda, looming up at an intersection, told Ash he'd wandered into Chinatown. Still he ambled on, down another narrow street, and came out upon the docks lining the East River. The salty air blowing in from seaward tugged at Tamerlane moving along one of the docks where stevedores were unloading a couple of sailing ships, one of Portugese registry, the larger one the schooner Galatea. Even here his clothing, erect carriage and cold set to his ruggedly-handsome features drew wondering eyes.

"Damn him for dying!" Tamerlane spat out to the choppy waters of the river. Now there'll be no way, he pondered, to tie Horace Eliot and others to the Cartel. The article in the *Times* had stated that Jason Webster had succumbed to a massive heart attack, and so it was highly unlikely he could have destroyed any ledgers or papers detailing his criminal activities. And a man who could so callously order others to do murder could also be blackmailing his business partners. This would mean more records. Which meant to Tamerlane he would attend the man's funeral scheduled for this afternoon, as would Frank O'Neal, in the hope that some of those coming to pay their last respects were some of those involved with the Cartel. And later tonight he would gain access to the Webster Building and the late Jason Webster's personal files.

"Can you spare a quid, guv'nor?"

Edging around, Ash stared back at a seaman hunched into a dark blue pea jacket, and curtly he replied, "Seems those stevedores could use some help."

"A bloody wiseguy!" snarled the man as he eased out a wicked-gleaming knife. "Hand over your cash, matey!"

Tamerlane's reaction was to sweep the bottom of his coat away and unleather the Deane-Adams. Without remorse a casual shot brought blood streaming from the man's hand, and as the sailor clutched at the wound, Ash simply strolled away past the startled eyes of those who'd witnessed the attempted robbery. And upon returning to Chinatown, he found the incident had taken his mind, if only temporarily, from what had brought him here, and put an edge to a hunger which carried him into a Chinese restaurant.

TWENTY-EIGHT

"Alright, cowboy, elevate your dukes and lean against that wall!"

Ash half-turned at the voice coming from behind him in the hallway, and then he saw another man coming out of Frank O'Neal's suite at the Astor Hotel.

Bunco squad Lieutenant Shawn Muldoon gestured to the other detective and said, "Easy, Conray. So you're Tamerlane?"

"And you most obviously are Muldoon."

"Lucky one of my men spotted Frank O'Neal down at the train depot. You don't know how good it makes me feel to see him again." A lopsided grin split Muldoon's wide lips. He was stocky, at five-ten a couple of inches shorter than Tamerlane, and had a ruddy complexion and light reddish hair cut short along the sides of his head. He would, Ash surmised, be a formidable adversary in a bar knuckle fight. "O'Neal's been telling me some cock and bull story about some hidden gold mine, and that Jason Webster and others are involved."

"It's the gospel, Lieutenant Muldoon."

"Just the same, Tamerlane, I'd like that revolver if you please." It was passed to him, whereupon Muldoon tossed it to the other detective. "I believe your father was the actor?"

"He was," Tamerlane nodded at his right breast pocket. "I've a letter here that might interest you." Under the waving gun of Lieutenant Muldoon, he removed an envelope from an inner coat pocket and passed it to Muldoon, then he moved between the detectives into the suite to find three more plainclothesmen watching the O'Neals.

"Isn't this overkill, lieutenant?"

Muldoon slid a finger under one end of the flap and tore the envelope open. "Frank O'Neal's the resourceful type."

"Your coming here," said Ash, "saves us a trip to your office."

"That so?" the lieutenant said dubiously as he stepped to a window letting in morning sunlight. The frown creased deeper into his forehead when he saw the official seal of territorial Montana stamped on the first page of the letter, and Sheriff Williams' scrawling signature. He skimmed over the contents of the four pages detailing the Cartel's western ventures, cast both Tamerlane and O'Neal skeptical glances, then swiped at his prominent nose while sorting out his thoughts.

"This," he finally muttered, "is dynamite! You three, go out and make some bunco arrests; Conray, wait in the hallway." He followed after his men leaving the suite and closed the door. "O'Neal, make me a drink—on second thought, fix us all one." He slapped the letter against the open palm of his left hand. "Jason Webster

234

is . . . or was, one of Manhattan's more prominent citizens. Gave generously to the police charity fund."

"He could afford to," Ash said dryly.

"According to what this letter details he sure as hell could. Dammit, Tamerlane, this is one hell of a situation."

"Nevertheless, it's all true. Webster ordered my family killed. And a lot of others. This will all come out in the trial. Sheriff Williams has sent telegrams to a lot of eastern newspapers requesting they send reporters."

"You forgot one important detail, Tamerlane."

"And that is?"

"Webster's dead; case closed!"

"He was the Cartel's chairman-of-the-board. Meaning there are more of Manhattan's social elite involved in this."

After O'Neal had passed to him a glass of brandy, Muldoon said, "Dammit, I've got a year until retirement. Now this." He gulped down the brandy, gestured for a refill. "And by the way, O'Neal, you blackmailed Horace Eliot, one of the men mentioned in this letter. What the hell am I gonna do about that? Nothing but throw you in the slammer."

"Let's suppose Frank turns state's evidence—"

Swiveling his gaze back to Ash, Lieutenant Muldoon said, "Like I just said, Tamerlane, only one year until I pull the pin. Hold off with this until then."

Now Ash also told O'Neal to refill his glass, and as Muldoon plopped down on a padded chair, Ash sat down facing the man. "Frank figured out the connection between Eliot and Jason Webster. We've got to pursue that."

"This . . . Cartel? What the hell does that mean? This

235

is New York, dammit, not cowpokey Montana." He slapped a meaty and decisive hand down at his knee. "But . . . you're right, crimes have been committed. O'Neal, you never introduced me to your wife—"

"Ah . . . this is Molly."

"Molly, whatever possessed you to marry this con artist?"

"He wanted to make me an honest woman. You see, Lieutenant Muldoon, I'm with child."

Frank O'Neal blinked at his wife, and Lieutenant Muldoon said, "How can I fight motherhood and the Catholic Church. Alright, alright, for the record, Mrs. O'Neal, your husband is as pure as driven snow. But, please, no hugs or the charge stands. O'Neal, dammit, another drink. I'll surely need it for what's to come."

"And what's that, lieutenant?"

"A search warrant, Tamerlane."

TWENTY-NINE

It was late afternoon, almost four o'clock, before Lieutenant Shawn Muldoon had convinced a lower court judge as to the validity of the letter presented to him by Ash Tamerlane. And so with a search warrant tucked into his coat pocket, he returned to the Astor Hotel and picked up Ash and Frank O'Neal.

Earlier, O'Neal had taken Ash up to Trinity Church situated at the north end of Wall Street and pointed out several prominent money men emerging from the church beind the ornate casket of the man Ash had come to kill, Jason Webster. Now, their hansom cab passing through streets on its way over to the Webster Building, it was the lieutenant voicing his worried opinion of the whole matter.

"I just hope no police officials are involved in this. If so, gents, I might as well turn in my badge now and forget about drawing any retirement pay." He blew an irritated smoke ring from his pudgy cigar at the two men seated facing him. "I'm handling this alone, just in case it comes to nothing."

"And if we come across incriminating documents in Webster's office?"

"Then I'll have no choice but to bring in the police commissioner's people." Twisting around on the seat, Muldoon shouted for the driver of their cab to drop them off in an alley passing alongside the soaring brick and steel building. Quickly he led Ash and O'Neal around and into the front entrance.

There, after finding the lobby was unattended, he produced a lock pick, and to Frank O'Neal's unmasked amusement, used it to gain access to the building. A wall directory listing the layout of the offices took them up to the fifth floor and into Jason Webster's suite of offices, a series of rooms facing toward the west and a pale sun pouring down cloud-filtered rays onto the Hudson River.

With the lieutenant converging on a shelf containing books and other papers and O'Neal wandering into another room, Ash stepped up to Webster's massive oaken desk. He rummaged through the drawers, came up with paperwork and bank books and bottles of medicine, but it was a call from O'Neal that gave them their first line to the Cartel. Hurrying into the adjoining room, both Ash and Lieutenant Muldoon scowled in puzzlement at a room containing only a few coat racks and a framed picture adorning the south wall.

"What the hell is this?"

"Seems to be an anteroom of some kind?"

"If it was a waiting room," questioned Muldoon, "there'd be some chairs?"

Ash stepped closer to the picture, and it suddenly dawned on him that here was a painting of some

238

mystical seal, perhaps that of the Cartel, for it showed a pyramid with a lidded eye in it and rays of light radiating downward from the pyramid to beam upon names etched into smaller pyramids, and he read, "Horace Eliot . . . R.L. Blackthorn . . ."

". . . Covington . . . James Sanborn?" Doffing his hat, Muldoon scratched worriedly at his receding hairline. "Some damned powerful names. Maybe, Tamerlane, it's just the names of Webster's board of directors. That pyramid . . . his company trademark or something."

Tamerlane probed with his fingers along the outside frame of the picture, and smiled at Muldoon when he came upon a recessed button, which he pressed to have a portion of the wall slide open revealing a large room containing a long table with five chairs around it. What held their attention as they entered the room was a larger replica of the painting they'd just viewed in the anteroom. The polished table top reflected Ash striding alongside it and the other men trailing. Just beyond the table, blotches of blood stained the plush green carpeting. A small, round, whitish capsule lying by the wall brought Ash over to pick it up and he said,

"What do you make of this?"

Around a shrug Muldoon said, "A nitroglycerin pill. Webster died from a heart attack. And in here, it seems."

"That blood indicates otherwise."

"Maybe."

O'Neal, upon noticing that the large painting seemed to be hanging slightly away from the wall, reached over to discover it was hinged at its other end, and he swung it away from the wall. He smiled at the vault door. "Seems, gentlemen, we've hit the mother lode."

Moving over, Lieutenant Muldoon jiggled the vault handle. "It's locked. Anyway all millionaires have vaults like this." He spun around and took off his hat and dropped it on the table. "Still, that blood could mean we have a situation here. Murder? Maybe. And knowing that James Sanborn is going to be our new police commissioner doesn't help my ulcer any. There's another thing; one of my men—"

Ash finished the sentence for the lieutenant, "Followed us here."

Grimacing to show his displeasure, Muldoon said, "Tamerlane, you seem to be the bright chap . . . so let's have your theory of what happened here."

Easing down to sit upon the table, Ash folded his arms across his chest and said, "I'll bet my three aces against your pair of deuces that a falling-out took place here. Webster hadn't been in the best of health, confined as he had been to a wheelchair. Knowing that he was dying, Webster could have called the others together . . . perhaps to dissolve his connection with the Cartel . . . or just to appoint someone else to take his place. This choice of his might have not set well with all of them. It even could be that Webster's doctor told the others he hadn't long to live. The bottom line among crooks, as you are aware, lieutenant, is men of this caliber don't like to share things."

"Just some damnable suppositions, Tamerlane."

"I'm wagering if you have Jason Webster's body exhumed, you'll find that his demise was caused by something other than a heart attack; this blood is witness to that, Muldoon. I'm also wagering you'll find another body in that vault."

240

"What are you, clairvoyant or something?"

"Just happened to notice this trail of blood over here." He went over and pointed at the floor.

Easing around O'Neal, the lieutenant crouched down beside Tamerlane and rubbed a finger at a small blotch of blood. "Yeah, it does seem like a body was dragged in there. But we know it isn't Jason Webster."

"You're the head of the bunco squad."

"Yeah?" Muldoon threw over his shoulder at Frank O'Neal.

"I know a safecracker who'd just love to get at this vault."

"So do I—in fact, several." Coming erect, he added, "Seems you just love breaking the law, O'Neal."

"Frank's right," cut in Ash. "I believe we'll find a lot of gold in there, and just possibly one of the late Jason Webster's business partners. Just maybe they won't want you to retire, lieutenant, if you break this thing open. You could be promoted to captain or inspector."

"Save the bullshine for us Irish," said Muldoon. "Okay, okay, there's this nitro pill, which by itself means nothing. But there's this blood . . . and gents, whoever caused it to be spilled plans to come back after the funeral and get at the contents of this vault. We're needing ourself a safecracker. And, O'Neal, one word from you that I availed myself of the services of a bunco artist and you'll rot in the slammer for life."

"Mums the word, lieutenant, as I'm planning on leaving for California to seek my fortune."

"And probably someone else's to boot. At least that cheers me some." Grabbing his hat, Lieutenant Muldoon hurried out of the conference room.

THIRTY

In the absence of Lieutenant Shawn Muldoon, Tamerlane had a chance to study the layout of the conference room, the heavy red broadloomed drapes covering the windows and opposite from the vault an ornately carved bar stocked with fine wines and imported liquors. But none of this show of pretentious wealth could downplay the faint mediciny scent clinging to the stuffy air or the aura of Jason Webster's sinister presence. It was here that Webster and his cronies plotted the murders of those he loved, outlined more schemes to men as soulless as he. It would be over soon, Tamerlane's long trail of vengence, and at the moment, lodged inside him, was this empty feeling.

He went over to where O'Neal had sat down on a stool at the bar and said, "Do you recall the names of the men on that painting, Frank?"

"Aye, I certainly do. Two of them, Covington and

Blackthorn, weren't at Webster's funeral. Do you really believe we'll find a body in that vault?"

"Like a man once said to me, there's some who'd gun you down for two bits. We're talking here of millions."

"Care for a drink?"

"Just some ice water," said Ash, and striding over, he touched the flame of a match to a couple of wall lamps hooded in expensive glass. Now the sound of footsteps passing along an outside corridor brought Ash swinging toward the open doorway, his hand going futilely to his empty holster. Then he smiled tautly when Lieutenant Muldoon came bouncing into the room trailed by two detectives escorting a man of seedy bearing and appearance. "Gallagher, the vault's back there; get to it." And shrugging out of his overcoat, Muldoon barked over at O'Neal, "I see you just can't keep away from the hard stuff."

"Can any Irishman pass up these bountiful delights?"

"Fix me one then," came back the lieutenant. "The temperature's really dropping . . . and what with everyone gone out of here for the weekend there's no way to get more heat into this room. It's damnwell Florida for me after I retire."

Through a fold in one of the curtains the lights of Manhattan seeped into the room, those lurking here expecting at any moment to be found out, until finally one of the detectives up by the vault exclaimed, "He's cracked it!"

Gathering near the vault door, the lieutenant stared anxiously at Ash Tamerlane as the safecracker stepped aside. "Go ahead, your cock-and-bull story brought us up here, open it."

Ash stepped forward and grasped the heavy metal handle worn smooth from constant use. Slowly he turned it sideways and swung the heavy vault door open, lamplight beaming from the conference room reaching out to touch the gleaming gold bars stacked in the vault and the lifeless forms of two men. Lining the vault walls were safe deposit boxes and shelves on which reposed jewelry and other precious items collected by Jason Webster. But it was chiefly the gold which carried Ash into the vault, and Muldoon and O'Neal.

"There must be millions in here."

"No wonder Jason Webster had to be killed."

"Too bad this gold can't talk."

"To my reckoning," said Ash, "it's stained with blood."

Frank O'Neal, after taking a closer look at the faces of the dead men, announced that they were indeed Covington and Blackthorn.

"Conray," barked the lieutenant, "I want those bodies taken to the morgue. But not a word as to where you found them. And you, Gallagher, for the time being you're gonna be a guest of the city."

"But, lieutenant—"

"Don't worry, I ain't bringing charges against you. But you gotta big mouth, Gallagher . . . and all I need right now is you spilling the beans about this to your cronies."

Later, after the bodies had been removed, O'Neal hefted one of the gold bars and grinned at Muldoon. "I might need some spare change."

Grinning back, Muldoon said, "Don't all of us. Now,

245

here's the way of it. Whoever did this will be back soon to remove those bodies . . . and I've a hunch it'll be tonight."

"My sentiments," Tamerlane said, as Lieutenant Muldoon dug the Deane-Adams out of a coat pocket and passed it over.

"And here, O'Neal, a gun for you," said the lieutenant. "Just be careful you don't shoot a big toe off." Closing and locking the vault door, he slid the painting back against the wall and joined the others by the bar.

Dousing the wall lamps, the door leading into the conference room having already been closed by one of the detectives, Tamerlane went over and opened some curtains so that nightlight shone into the room. At the bar, he sat down on a high stool and gazed at Frank O'Neal for a long moment.

"You're come a long way, Frank."

"I've a feeling, Ash, you've still got another river to cross."

"You speaking about Wyomia?"

"She's a part of it."

"Hey," said Lieutenant Muldoon, "I hear something? Yeah, someone's in the next room." He slipped behind the bar with the others and palmed his service revolver. "Remember, we let whoever it is open the vault first."

Palming his Deane-Adams, Ash Tamerlane felt a tremor of anxiety mingled with anger rising to film his eyes. He felt cheated by Jason Webster's unexpected death. But at work in Ash was a shard of conscience telling him to still this impulse to kill.

The door to the north slid open, and someone

246

bearing a lamp entered to pass along the wall running toward the vault. Halfway along the conference table, he paused to light a wall lamp as another man hurried into the room pulling a handcart, and this man said, "Horace, I hope you managed to get the right combination."

"Don't worry, James, it's the right one. Just think, Webster's no longer around to get the lion's share of the gold. The Cartel is ours now."

"I'm through with that crooked business, Horace."

"With the Cartel? Look what it's given us."

"For me it's been a lot of sleepless nights. Gold isn't everything."

"Gold is everything," said Horace Eliot in a quivering voice. "It's power, the world." With a sorrowful shake of his head for Sanborn, Eliot turned and hurried over to pull the painting away from the wall. Setting the lamp he carried on the floor, he busied himself with the vault door. His smothered curse when he bungled that first attempt to open the vault carried plainly across the room.

"Ahh, there you have it," exulted James Sanborn, distinguished by an erect carriage and grey streaking the black hair, whereas Eliot was a paunchy man with a fawning smile. He picked up the lamp from the floor as the door was swung open by Eliot, and suddenly Sanborn had reeled back a step. "What is this?"

The other member of the Cartel now glanced into the vault, and he cried out in fear, "Someone's stumbled onto our little game!" But Horace Eliot still couldn't comprehend that those they'd murdered could be anyplace but in this vault. He spun on his partner while pulling out a handgun. "You're the only one who knew about this." There was panic in his voice now. "You know all of it . . . where all of the bodies are buried . . . damn you."

"Pull yourself together, Horace. I was with you, remember, ever since this happened."

"This is the police!" Lieutenant Muldoon. "Drop your weapons and surrender!"

Flame gushed from Horace Eliot's revolver, and James Sanborn screamed out in pain and disbelief. A second slug from his partner's gun sent him falling limply to the flor.

"There," Eliot said wildly, "now it's all mine. The Cartel . . . the gold . . . all mine." His hand falling limply at his side but still clutching the handgun, he seemed unaware of those rushing past the table as he turned around slowly and blundered into the vault. Fondly he reached out and stroked a hand along a gold bar. "We shall have to bring in new members. Perhaps this time they'll make me chairman of the Cartel." He smiled at the stacks of gleaming golden bars. "Pretty, aren't you . . . and yet so very, very deadly—"

Closing in on the open vault door, Tamerlane brought up the Deane-Adams and centered it on Horace Eliot's back, his finger tightening on the trigger, wanting desperately to kill, and somehow answering the pleading gaze in the eyes of Frank O'Neal. Abruptly, he lowered his arm. "Lucky for Eliot he went over the deep edge. As I almost did."

Both men stood there as Lieutenant Muldoon walked calmly into the vault and took the gun from Horace Eliot. And O'Neal said softly, tiredly, "I can't believe it's over, Ash. By rights some of that gold is

248

yours, since your father invested a lot of money with the Cartel."

"Maybe some of it is, Frank. But I'm not sticking around to claim it. Take care . . . and I hope you make it big out west, my friend." Then he was gone, leaving behind the gold and all of its blood-stained memories.

THIRTY-ONE

It was the third day before Christmas and the sound of sleigh bells came melodiously to Ash Tamerlane seated in the front seat of a carriage being pulled by a curried black horse. Huge crystalline snowflakes fell lazily around him, and in the masions he passed on East 36th Street, lights called out a yuletide greeting.

The sensational trial of Horace Eliot had shocked New York City and the nation. Eliot's revelations had, in turn, brought more arrests. Through it all Ash was there, mainly because of a subpeona personally delivered to him by Lieutenant Muldoon. Others participating in the trial had been thc O'Neals, and from Montana had come Sheriff Jim Williams, along with folks from Colorado. Later had come the settling of claims brought against the Cartel, and much to Tamerlane's surprise he had been awarded a considerable amount of money. And then at last he'd been free to go.

Last night had found Ash boarding a train at Grand Central Station with every intention of heading west again. He'd stared out of a window in his sleeping car, torn by what this city and Wyomia Blair had once meant to him. Then, impulsively, he had collected his baggage and returned to the Astor Hotel. The Xmas present reclining on the seat next to him had also been an impulsive whim, for he had suddenly realized he must go and see Wyomia and beg her forgiveness for the dark thoughts he'd been harboring about her, and just to gaze once again at the only woman he had ever loved.

For the occasion he'd decked himself out in a fashionable suit, a stylish fur coat and hat, and now with a great deal of apprehension he reined the black into a long winding driveway lined with trimmed aspen trees. As he drew up before the wide stairs of the front entrance, a servant came out of a side door and took charge of Ash's horse.

Climbing out of the carriage, he said, "Nice evening."

"It is, sir."

"Is Wyomia in residence?"

"Yes, but she's leaving for the Continent tomorrow."

"Obliged," replied Ash as he hurried up the marble steps to have a butler open the front door.

"If you're here, sir, to see Mr. Culver I'm afraid he isn't home."

"Will you please tell Mrs. Wyomia Blair that Ash Tamerlane is calling on her."

"Tamerlane? I remember you from before? Certainly . . . Mr. Tamerlane." He closed the door behind Ash and hurried up a curving staircase.

When at least twenty minutes had passed and there was no sign of Wyomia, Ash realized it had been a mistake coming here. Wistfully he went over and placed the Christmas present he'd bought her on the staircase, and on the verge of turning, chanced to glance upward, finding her staring down at him from the second-floor landing.

Wyomia said quietly, "I knew someday you'd come back, Ash Tamerlane."

"You did?"

She started down the staircase. "Always."

"I . . . I've never stopped . . . loving you—"

Now she stood within arm's-length and murmured, "I know, Ash. I can see it in your eyes."

"You came west looking for me."

"But you're here now. Must I look any further?"

Tamerlane's response was to reach for Wyomia's hand. Drawing her close, he said, "Afraid I'm not the same man you once knew."

"You're a better man, Ash—my man."

There was no need to say any more.

BEST OF THE WEST
from Zebra Books

THOMPSON'S MOUNTAIN   (2042, $3.95)
by G. Clifton Wisler

Jeff Thompson was a boy of fifteen when his pa refused to sell out his mountain to the Union Pacific and got gunned down in return, along with the boy's mother. Jeff fled to Colorado, but he knew he'd even the score with the railroad man who had his parents killed . . . and either death or glory was at the end of the vengeance trail he'd blaze!

BROTHER WOLF   (1728, $2.95)
by Dan Parkinson

Only two men could help Lattimer run down the sheriff's killers—a stranger named Stillwell and an Apache who was as deadly with a Colt as he was with a knife. One of them would see justice done—from the muzzle of a six-gun.

BLOOD ARROW   (1549, $2.50)

by Dan Parkinson
Randall Kerry returned to his camp to find his companion slaughtered and scalped. With a war cry as wild as the savages,' the young scout raced forward with his pistol held high to meet them in battle.

THUNDERLAND   (1991, $3.50)
by Dan Parkinson

Men were suddenly dying all around Jonathan, and he needed to know why—before he became the next bloody victim of the ancient sword that would shape the future of the Texas frontier.

APACHE GOLD   (1899, $2.95)
by Mark K. Roberts & Patrick E. Andrews
Chief Halcon burned with a fierce hatred for the pony soldiers that rode from Fort Dawson, and vowed to take the scalp of every round-eye in the territory. Sergeant O'Callan must ride to glory or death for peace on the new frontier.

Available wherever paperbacks are sold, or order direct from the Publisher. Send cover price plus 50¢ per copy for mailing and handling to Zebra Books, Dept. 2333, 475 Park Avenue South, New York, N.Y. 10016. Residents of New York, New Jersey and Pennsylvania must include sales tax. DO NOT SEND CASH.

BOLD HEROES OF THE UNTAMED NORTHWEST!
THE SCARLET RIDERS
by Ian Anderson

#1: CORPORAL CAVANNAGH   (1161, $2.50)
Joining the Mounties was Cavannagh's last chance at a new life. Now he would stop either an Indian war, or a bullet — and out of his daring and courage a legend would be born!

#2: THE RETURN OF CAVANNAGH   (1817, $2.25)
A private army of bloodthirsty outlaws are hired to massacre the Mounties at Fort Walsh. Joined by the bold Indian fighter Cavannagh, the Riders prepare for the deadliest battle of their lives!

#3: BEYOND THE STONE HEAPS   (1884, $2.50)
Fresh from the slaughter at the Little Big Horn, the Sioux cross the border into Canada. Only Cavannagh can prevent the raging Indian war that threatens to destroy the Scarlet Riders!

#4: SERGEANT O'REILLY   (1977, $2.50)
When an Indian village is reduced to ashes, Sergeant O'Reilly of the Mounties risks his life and career to help an avenging Stoney chief and bring a silver-hungry murderer to justice!

#5: FORT TERROR   (2125, $2.50)
Captured by the robed and bearded killer monks of Fort Terror, Parsons knew it was up to him, and him alone, to stop a terrifying reign of anarchy and chaos by the deadliest assassins in the territory — and continue the growing legend of The Scarlet Riders!